Megan looked him straight in the eye as she took her seat.

And the expression there...the compassion, the sorrow...stopped the angry words about to escape his lips.

"I'm pregnant, Danny. I didn't mean to have this conversation here. I just found out last night. Wanted to wait to tell you in person, but not like this. Then the lobster...and... I'm so sorry."

Her apology dashed his anger, leaving him with a cacophony of thoughts and emotions swirling into a confusing fog.

"You're sorry that you're pregnant? Or that it's my baby?" That apology. It was there. He had a hold of it.

"I'm sorry that you're in the position of father-to-be when I know it's the absolute last thing you want for your life. When you've expressly chosen not to be a man with a family because you know it's the best and happiest route for you to take for yourself and for others."

He didn't need her psychiatry talk.

He needed his friend.

Dear Reader,

Welcome back to Sierra's Web, the firm of experts who solve problems, help with family dilemmas and fight crime, too! Megan and Daniel are best friends from college who both work for Sierra's Web and they're together on a case, and I'm envious that you get to be there with them for the first time. I've been there several times by now, but each time, I get *that* feeling!

I write romance because I believe in that feeling. I know that it's real. That love exists. That in its purest form, it can heal any hurts, and that it has the power to win, every time. Not just romantic love, but friend love, family love, all love. Love lives in all of us and is our greatest strength, our greatest protection against evil.

And having an übersexy best friend...well, that's just a bonus!

Tara Taylor Quinn

Her Best Friend's Baby

TARA TAYLOR QUINN

HARLEQUIN
SPECIAL
EDITION

HARLEQUIN®
SPECIAL EDITION™

Recycling programs for this product may not exist in your area.

ISBN-13: 978-1-335-72438-0

Her Best Friend's Baby

Copyright © 2022 by TTQ Books LLC

For questions and comments about the quality of this book, please contact us at CustomerService@Harlequin.com.

Harlequin Enterprises ULC
22 Adelaide St. West, 41st Floor
Toronto, Ontario M5H 4E3, Canada
www.Harlequin.com

Printed in U.S.A.

Having written over ninety novels, **Tara Taylor Quinn** is a *USA TODAY* bestselling author with more than seven million copies sold. She is known for delivering intense, emotional fiction. Tara is a past president of Romance Writers of America and a seven-time RITA® Award finalist. She has also appeared on TV across the country, including *CBS Sunday Morning*. She supports the National Domestic Violence Hotline. If you need help, please contact 1-800-799-7233.

Books by Tara Taylor Quinn

Harlequin Special Edition

Sierra's Web

His Lost and Found Family
Reluctant Roommates

The Parent Portal

Having the Soldier's Baby
A Baby Affair
Her Motherhood Wish
A Mother's Secrets
The Child Who Changed Them
Their Second-Chance Baby
Her Christmas Future

The Daycare Chronicles

Her Lost and Found Baby
An Unexpected Christmas Baby
The Baby Arrangement

The Fortunes of Texas

Fortune's Christmas Baby

Visit the Author Profile page
at Harlequin.com for more titles.

Chapter One

A wedding was happening.

Sitting alone in the back of a cab, on her way to the hotel that would be her home away from home for the next bit, Megan Latimer stopped the train of thought, stiffened her spine, refused to wallow.

What did it matter that a whole group of her friends were there, and she wasn't? Really, was she going to play a "poor me" card? Feeling all sad and lonely and pathetic? Like she couldn't be laughing and celebrating at the afternoon destination wedding at the all-inclusive, adults-only resort in Jamaica if she wanted to be?

Okay, well, reality check; she couldn't actually be at that particular wedding celebration.

She hadn't been invited.

After all, the groom wouldn't generally invite his ex-fiancée to his fancy dancy, three-day-long nuptial celebration on the beach. Especially when they'd been broken up for just six months.

And therein lay the rub. Megan had been with Kurt for three years. Had been engaged for half that time. And he'd never even been willing to talk seriously about setting a wedding date, let alone delving into any kind of actual wedding plans.

Yet six months after their breakup, he was married to someone else?

She checked her watch. Three twenty-five. The extravagant, romantic ceremony had been scheduled for three, and her phone would have blown up if it hadn't happened.

As the shops and bars and office buildings of downtown Milwaukee flew past in a blur, Megan sat stiffly, hands folded atop the gray dress pants she wore with the white long-sleeved cotton shirt and gray, black-and-white sweater and reminded herself that she'd been as ready as Kurt was to end their relationship. It was time to turn her focus to what did matter—the job ahead and the family who'd hired her for her expertise in pediatric psychiatry. They needed her to help save their seventeen-year-old daughter from what they claimed was abusive mental manipulation by the teen's boyfriend and his mother.

Megan had a new challenge ahead. Married ex-fiancé or no.

Her newest client was a young woman, Samantha Everson, who claimed to be in love with her boyfriend and wanted to live with him and his mother.

Lindy and Joe Everson, her parents, were panicked at the change they'd seen in their daughter. With the help of expert consultants, renowned child and family court lawyer Daniel Tremaine, and Megan, the Eversons were intending to petition the court to force Sammie to live at home. Megan, who was privy to medical records, knew Samantha was newly pregnant. Danny didn't yet.

The law was on their side: Wisconsin mandated that children live with their parent or legal guardian until the age of eighteen.

Not that Megan had to worry about state law. Danny would handle all of the court stuff. He'd work his magic. Rely on her opinion as to what was best for Samantha—then get things done.

And…relax.

Just the thought of her best friend had her chest easing, her back sinking into the car seat rather than sitting rigidly against it, and her smile finding its way out.

Danny. Quintessential ladies' man. The guy every one of her sorority sisters in college wanted to sleep with. Except cute little blond-headed Megan.

A lot of them had had their one time doing it with

Danny. But Megan had had the last laugh. She was the only one still in touch with him. She had the real man. The Danny no other woman knew. Her kind, funny, easy-on-the-eyes best friend.

Daniel Tremaine. The hotshot lawyer who had answers for everything.

In a few short hours, she'd be looking into those big blue eyes, seeing herself there, finding her sense of humor, and her mojo, too.

Even if her ex-fiancé had just married someone else…life was good.

"Can I get you anything else, sir?" The words themselves were sedate. Commonplace. Had been said all up and down the plane's too skinny aisle. But the sultry tone of voice, the appreciative look in the woman's seductive gaze, the clearly welcoming smile, told him quite clearly what she'd like to offer him.

What she *was* offering, if he wanted it.

"No, thanks." Danny flashed a smile, softening the rejection, and turned back to his computer. He'd have to shut down soon and wanted to get through the legal brief, so he'd have all night free.

It was a stroke of good luck that he'd managed to get on an earlier flight, and no way he was giving up time he got to spend with Megan—even to go have sex. Physical pleasure was great and something that had never been in short supply for him, or from him, either—but a whole evening to spend with the woman who was a friend not lover…that was rare. No way he was going to let that slip away.

What did it say about him that a sexless evening with Megan ranked far higher than going to bed with a beautiful woman?

He didn't really want an answer to that question. And as soon as he deplaned, collected their rental car and found the hotel, he texted Megan.

Here. Got an early flight. Meet you in the bar?

And grinned at the immediateness of her reply.

On my way.

"Is there something wrong with me?" Megan heard how pathetic the question sounded but didn't care. Danny was the only one who'd heard it.

The number of rum and diets she'd had to drink—less than him, though—probably had something to do with her lack of remorse as well. At the moment she didn't much care about that, either.

She and Danny had been drinking and philosophizing, sharing secrets, since their freshman year in college.

Almost a decade and a half ago. "I'm thirty-one, not married, with no prospects on the horizon," she continued before he could answer. He was her friend. But he'd also tell her if there was something wrong with her, and she was in no state to hear about it. "Hell, I don't even have a horizon," she continued, looking down into her drink in case she might find one there. A horizon. Or a prospect.

Neither appeared.

She needed to call it a night. Get her sorry ass into bed and awake in the morning with her usual strength and positive attitude.

"It's not you, Meg." Danny's serious, but also vulnerable, tone was the one that had drawn her to him in college. The one that she trusted most. The one that most people never heard.

That tone was why she'd first given the guy voted "most desirable hunk on campus" the time of day. Prior to him coming to her one night at a party, late, completely sober and asking her opinion, she'd steered as clear of him as campus, and both being part of Greek life, had allowed.

Over the course of their undergraduate career, the dark-haired, blue-eyed, gorgeous-bodied man had come to her for advice many times. It wasn't just about the women who hung on him because of his abundantly good looks and popularity, but about life, about being the best person he could be, about ways to not hurt people, not run them over, in pursuit of his own goals.

She'd been his therapist. He'd opened up to her even before she'd actually attained her M.D. in psychiatry.

And in his own way, he'd been hers.

She could always count on Danny to be honest with her. Even when it hurt.

"What does that mean, it's not me?" She didn't want to know. She wanted to go to bed. Or have another drink and hang out with her best friend for a little bit longer, laughing. She wanted Danny to make her laugh again. Like they'd been doing most of the night. Remembering ridiculous stuff. Catching up with things that they hadn't covered in their weekly phone conversations.

This was their only downtime, and they both knew it. Once the job started in the morning, they'd both be so focused…working in their off-hours. They were two peas in a pod, work-wise, which was why they got so many assignments together.

She should never have started this stupid conversation. "You want another?" she asked when she saw the waitress heading their way. Sloppy, maybe, but still a change of subject.

"If you do." She nodded at him, he nodded at the waitress, and then he said, "You're special, Meg. In the best way. The guy who finally gets you…he's going to be one lucky dude. But he's going to have to be special, too, to deserve you. To make you happy. Kurt was fine, nice enough, but he wasn't special."

With a grimace, she pushed aside the no longer cold liquid in her glass, waiting for the fresh drink on its way, and met his gaze. "That's a nice way of saying I'm high maintenance," she told him.

His scoff couldn't be mistaken for anything but the honest sense of scorn that it was. "Yeah right," he said. "You're the lowest maintenance woman I've ever met. And that's why it's going to take a special guy to make you happy. You need someone who's happy on his own when you're off doing what you do, someone who needs to be himself and who is strengthened by you being yourself, and someone who, even if you're not in each other's pockets all the time, will always be faithful to you."

Yep, there it was. The real rub. The thing she hadn't let herself consciously acknowledge.

Of course, Danny would bring it up. He knew her better than she knew herself sometimes.

"So, you think it, too... Kurt was having a thing with her when he and I were living together. No way he'd be married so soon if he hadn't been unfaithful to me."

Infidelity was her bugaboo. The emotional trigger she couldn't seem to disarm. And Danny knew why without her ever having to tell him. He'd been there the day their first year when her parents had shown up and told her they were divorcing. She, her mom and her dad been the three musketeers until her teen years, when everything had fallen apart. She hadn't even known there'd been a problem. They put on the perfect face for her. She'd been sure it was her. Instead, her perfect parents, the loving couple who'd always been there for her, had been living a lie. Because one of them had been unfaithful to the other. They'd never told her which one.

She'd asked. Each of them separately. More than once.

And still didn't know.

They'd both remarried, childless spouses, and she had a great relationship with both of them and both stepparents. Was loved and adored as the only child of both families.

And she still would rather be single forever than have a family implode because of infidelity.

"I thought Kurt would be the last man on earth who'd be unfaithful," she said, looking for the waitress who should be arriving with her drink. She'd like a sip. Or three.

"Which is why you were with him, right?" The drinks arrived. The waitress placed Megan's in front of her.

"Not completely!" She sipped. "I mean, yeah, I loved that about him, his integrity, his noninterest in any woman but me because I made him happy, I was enough for him, the way he liked to spend his free time at home, even before he knew me…"

"He was boring, Meg. And a bit lazy, too, if you ask me."

She felt a smile coming up, but it died before it

reached the surface. "He worked hard. Made a good living."

"He's got a brilliant mind and happened to be one of the best techies in the country," Danny said, his singing of Kurt's praises raising her ire for no fair reason. "It's pretty clear he made good money. But he didn't work hard. The man worked about six hours a day, from anything I ever heard, and then he fooled around and basically hung out. With his mind, he could have been solving internet crime issues, putting a stop to hacking, or at the very least, inventing new cool video games…"

Okay, that was better.

"He made more money than I do." She had to give the token defense.

"And that's what you judge a man by these days?"

Shocked, she stared at him.

"I loved him," she defended but heard the weakness in her tone. She might be able to fool herself, but she couldn't lie to Danny. She shook her head. "So, okay, maybe I didn't. Not like he needed to be loved. But he could have come to me, talked to me about our relationship, before hooking up with someone else behind my back."

"Completely agree with you on that one." Taking a sip of the dark-colored liquid in his glass, Danny sat back, gorgeous in his thinly stripped white shirt, haphazardly unbuttoned at the neck, with the knot on his red tie loosened down past the second shirt button. The suit jacket he'd had on when she'd first seen him was slung over the back of the booth beside him.

"What?" he asked as she stared at him pensively.

"Nothing," she said, shaking her head. Yeah, Danny was gorgeous. Easily the best-looking guy she'd ever seen. *And* the least likely to ever be faithful to any woman.

Which made him unattractive to her in any kind of a sexual way.

"What?" he asked again, more forcefully, his lips tilted into that smile that got women to swoon on a regular basis. And Danny, being there, the gentleman willing to ease their pangs.

He never promised anything he didn't deliver, though. From what she'd heard, he was as good in bed as he looked like he would be.

And he always made it clear, from the outset of any tryst, that he wasn't open to anything more than an enjoyable time for however long it lasted.

"You," she said out loud.

"What about me?"

Shaking her head, she swooned for a second, alcohol induced, she knew, sipped again anyway, and said, "I have no idea why we became friends."

"Seriously?" He looked hurt.

Which hadn't been her intention at all.

"More accurately, I don't know why you chose to be friends with me." As a woman who only wanted sex on a committed, monogamous basis, she'd been dumbfounded the first time he'd sought her out.

They'd been at a combined sorority-frat Christmas party. As a freshman pledge, he'd been designated driver and had taken the responsibility with complete seriousness. He'd been drinking soda all night. She'd been sober because she'd had a late-night flight to catch to her dad's place in California, before heading to her mom's in Florida for the actual holiday. At first when he'd started a conversation with her, she hadn't even known he was speaking to her...

Danny's blue gaze grabbed her. Held her attention. The intensity she read in his grown-up eyes startled her. "Truth?" he asked.

Almost as though mesmerized, she nodded. She couldn't not. She'd always wondered...wasn't ever sure she wanted to know. Had been afraid to find out.

And there they were...on some kind of precipice, like a new level to their friendship. She wasn't afraid anymore.

"Because you were the only woman I knew on campus who found my thoughts more attractive than my body."

Elation-like sensation rushed through her. And a wealth of love, too.

Relief in huge measure.

She'd expected to hear that he hadn't meant to even talk to her that night, that he had just been being polite.

"I did," she said, nodding, holding his gaze. "I still do." Were they really going to do this? To talk about their relationship?

There hadn't ever been words about *it*.

Before she could analyze the wisdom or healthiness in such a move, Megan opened her mouth again, inspired by alcohol, to say things she maybe had wanted to say before. To verbalize what she knew to see what he thought about it.

"You're my soul mate, Danny. Like we were meant to be friends because we meet on some deeper level." She gulped, literally from her glass, as soon as the words were out. Forcing herself to look at him, to assess the damage she'd just done, and then, when she saw the serious, but open expression on his face, tried to assess how drunk he was.

She failed on that one. And said, "I trust you as much as I trust my own thoughts."

"Yeah, I trust you, too," he told her, sounding as though he'd just tried on the idea, and liked how well it fit.

She wasn't sure how many drinks he'd had before she arrived in the bar. Or how many he'd had since. He was a responsible drinker, as was she. Neither of them was slurring their words.

But she wasn't feeling any pain, either.

Really? She was going to sit there at such a crucial moment and analyze her buzz?

"You know when you were little, before your parents decided they hated each other, and you'd look under the tree on Christmas morning, see all those presents, and the sparkly colored lights, that feeling you'd get in your stomach?"

He'd told her about the two Christmases he could remember as a kid, before his home had turned into World War III, the war to end all wars, except it hadn't ever ended. His parents, who cared more about the lifestyle they could maintain together than living with someone they actually enjoyed, were still together.

"Yeah," he said, not quite frowning, but looking a bit perplexed. "That was a great feeling."

"Kind of like magic," she agreed, remembering many, many more of those Christmases in her own youth. "Like the possibilities were endless, and every one of them good."

"Yeah." He cocked his head to the side in a way that she'd always secretly liked. It was warm. Human. And not at all a come-on. His smile was natural, too. "Exactly."

"That's how I feel when I know I'm going to see you," she said. "Or when I see your name pop up on my caller ID. Or hear your voice pick up when I call you."

She'd bared herself. Risking that he was as much of a soul mate as she'd thought.

Analyzing the buzz might have been a wiser idea.

She was going to lose him at some point. She'd

always known that. Just stood to reason that some-day some woman was going to be able to offer him friendship and sex at the same time. And when that happened, he wouldn't need Megan as much.

More likely, the woman wouldn't accept Megan as part of the package.

Funny, how Kurt hadn't ever minded Danny in her life.

But maybe her ex-fiancé had never been in love with her, either...

"You want to dance?"

She blinked. Sat back. Stared at him.

There was some soft music. A small dance floor. Couples had been on and off it all night.

She and Danny weren't a couple.

"Haven't you ever opened a Christmas present and found something you didn't expect, but ended up being glad you got?"

"Danny..." What the hell. Had she said too much? Ruined things between them?

"Relax, Latimer, just trying to be a good soul mate here. You're in a funk because of the dancing and celebrating going on down south on some beach. You love to dance. Maybe even need to dance a little bit tonight, you know, work off some of that alcohol, and you aren't a woman who'd risk a stranger's arms. I'm fairly good at dancing. And safe."

It wasn't like they'd never danced before. To the contrary, he'd been her "date" at both of her parents' weddings during college. Had spent the evenings making her laugh. And helping her feel less abandoned.

And she got what he was doing. In his own way, Danny had just told her that she was his Christmas magic, too. Ha. Who'd have guessed that Christmas in July really did happen?

Chapter Two

What in the hell was he doing? Holding Megan close, feeling the push of her breasts against his chest, feeling her breath on his neck…

Unable to throw his hands up and back away as every instinct in his body was telling him to do, he swayed slowly to some instrumental version of a love song from the nineties.

He could count the times on one hand that Meg had been as vulnerable as she was that night. The way she'd been questioning herself…had kind of unsettled him, truth be known. Meg was the one with the answers not the questions.

Even when she did have questions, she asked them with the confidence of knowing she could deal with the answer. But minutes before, in the booth...not so much.

She needed more than just words. And he'd die before he turned away from Megan Latimer in a time of need. So he danced. Held her in the only way he could.

Fought his instincts with everything he had. Because just as they were telling him to get away from Megan Latimer's body, another side of him knew exactly how to help her feel exquisitely better. Making women feel good was a particular talent of his. Something he'd apparently been born with.

A blessing.

And a curse.

He wasn't sure which it was as she stumbled against him. His arms tightened automatically as his body supported hers, and when she burped softly, then giggled, he laughed, too. Infected by her funny bone, he couldn't help himself, his body bubbling with humor, against hers.

"Remember when the guys used to have those gross burping contests?" she asked, her words not quite slurred, but getting close in the way she drew them out.

"I'd rather forget," he told her, grinning in spite of himself.

"You never won."

"I never played."

"I know. You were too cool to burp." Her bright

gaze peered up at him, happiness shining through the teasing.

Her pleasure pleased him. He was succeeding in his goal. Being a particularly good soul mate.

"I can't burp on demand," he said quite seriously.

Her guffaw of laughter drew eyes from another couple sharing the small floor. He hoped they liked what they saw—him and Megan having fun together.

How could that not make a good picture?

"Yeah, right." She leaned into him a bit more. He took her weight willingly.

"I can't," he told her, eyes wide. It was one of his embarrassing secrets. One he'd never shared with anyone. "I practiced. You have no idea how hard I practiced. Starting in grade school. What kind of guy can't burp, you know?"

Leaning back, she peered up at him, her eyes a bit squinted—and her lower body pressing against his with the movement.

Oooo boy.

"You seriously can't make yourself burp?"

He shook his head. *Burping. Think about burping.*

"I tried all the tricks," he distantly recalled.

"Like what?" Her chin knocked his chest as looked up at him.

And her grin roiled his insides. "Sucking in air and drinking water on top of it for one. You know, to trap the air…"

She hissed in air. And he knew.

She'd felt what he'd been trying so hard to prevent.

His penis was hard.

For her.

Now was the time for karma to swoop in and knock him dead.

Hard penis.

On the dance floor.

"It's just an involuntary reaction," she said aloud. In case anyone needed confirmation.

Danny didn't say a word. Just kept swaying with her to the music.

"I'm a doctor. I know these things," she confirmed for good measure.

And...the music stopped.

Panic struck for a second. Illogical emotion that she curtailed before giving it a second thought. But... "You want to finish our last drink before we go up?"

"I could use it." Danny's voice sounded odd.

The whole penis thing, she was sure.

Sucked being a guy sometimes.

"I'm having fun," she declared as they slid back into their respective sides of the booth. "I knew I would. I knew as soon as I saw you, I'd find my fun again."

"I thought you needed your soul mate."

"Yeah, that, too," she said, growing serious as she looked across at him. "I didn't screw things up by saying that, did I?" she asked, pushing her drink away rather consuming anymore. She was pretty buzzed.

"I hope I didn't. If I did, just cancel it."

Maybe life could be that easy. Once in a lifetime, at least. Please.

"You ready to go up?" he asked, and she panicked again. Because…maybe she really had crossed a line. Oh, God, what if…she couldn't contemplate life without her friend…

But, she stood. It was the right thing to do. Waited while he paid the tab. It was his turn. She'd get the next one.

At least that was going right. Normally.

In the elevator, it all fell apart again. She stood on one side, he leaned a shoulder against the wall of the other. They both stared at the numbers above the door, watching the light flick from one floor to the next.

Come on twelve. They were on twelve. In adjoining rooms.

So they could meet for the case.

She'd seen a bellman bringing his bags up as she'd left to go down and meet him in the bar.

Hours ago.

Felt like a lifetime.

She had to fix this. Racked her alcohol-numbed brain for the expertise that helped people all over the country.

"Physicians shouldn't try to heal themselves," she

mumbled aloud, though she hadn't done so intentionally.

"That's what I've heard," he replied.

Were they making polite conversation? Nonsensical words because neither of them was in a state to make much sense?

Or had they just agreed that she couldn't fix what she'd broken?

Twelve. The light struck, stayed, the bell dinged and the door opened.

Her door was first. He could enter his room through it. But she stood outside, key card in hand. Looked up at him and couldn't stop the tears that sprang to her eyes. "I can't lose you, Danny."

"Hey, what's this?" Bending enough to look her straight in the eye while his thumb rubbed her cheek, catching a tear as it fell. "You aren't going to lose me, Meg. What kind of talk is that?"

"I just…it felt so good, just to be held for a second, you know? It didn't mean anything. Just…it's been a bad day. My fault because I let the whole marriage-so-quick nonsense get to me. I should have just had dinner sent up, but it was you and you know…"

His nod seemed so sure. So right. And in control.

When she was melting into a puddle right there in the hall.

"You were right to come down," he said. "I'd have been…hurt…if you hadn't. It's us. Mopping up tears is something we're best at. It's what friends...no... what soul mates are for."

He must have had more to drink than she'd realized. Danny's tenderness was nothing new. The words...not his style.

Danny had a way of letting you know he understood, while making light of things so you could get out of the muck and laugh at yourself. At someone else. Laugh at the whole damned world if that was what it took.

"I'm going to be just fine."

"I know."

"I didn't love him."

"I know that, too."

"I thought I did."

"Yeah."

Right, they'd been over all that. After the third or fourth drink.

"I'd be all right now if I hadn't had too much to drink..."

"Maybe. Or maybe you'd have just suppressed it all, and I have it on exceptionally good authority that suppression isn't healthy." His smile brought hers up out of her puddle of woe.

"Oh yeah? On what authority?" Sticking her chin up a little too quickly, she lost a bit of balance, braced herself with a hand against his chest and knocked her nose into his jaw anyway. He turned his head, seemingly to try to avoid the collision that had already taken place, and she didn't pull back quickly enough.

His lips grazed hers.

Soft heat against…wow…were her lips really that starved for affection? That they just stuck there? And why not? She was in need.

And Danny…he was Danny. Safe. Her friend.

Ready to take one on the chin for her.

And so damned hot.

A real man.

He'd been hard.

For her.

Wow.

His lips touched hers again.

She liked it.

Kissed him with hunger.

Someone used her key to open her door. Maybe her. She couldn't remember doing it, but somehow it opened and they kind of fell inside.

Still kissing.

And then…the bed was right there. They really needed to lie down.

And to quit thinking.

Chapter Three

Sheets moved. Waking him. Someone getting up. Had he hooked up with the flight attendant after all? Had she followed him to...

Oh God. No. Oh God.

It wasn't the flight attendant.

Fully awake, he lay still, barely breathing.

The bar.

Megan.

Drinks.

Dancing.

Were there burps?

Tears. Definitely tears.

Hard on.

Oh God.

Oh God.

Oh God.

He heard the rustling. Was experienced enough to know she was getting dressed. To go where? They were in her room.

Weren't they?

He didn't dare open his eyes to find out. Wasn't ready to face her.

Oh God.

What in the hell had he done?

He needed to die right then and there.

Except she'd have to explain a dead body in her bed.

So, he'd wait for her to go wherever she was going, slip into his own room and slit his throat.

Well, not that. Too messy.

No way he was going to check out on her, in any case.

But a guy could dream, couldn't he? Even if he was just feigning sleep?

A door closed. He heard water running.

And realized that Megan hadn't been getting dressed to go somewhere. She'd been collecting whatever she needed to take a shower.

He hoped.

Not sure that he'd have more than a minute or two, he flew out of bed, grabbed his pants. Put them on inside out. Grabbed the rest of his belongings one by one off the floor, and curtailed it out of there.

In his own room, he realized he was missing a

sock. Threw its mate in the trash. And just before he got in the shower, sent a text to Meg.

Coffee at seven? We need to go over the case before the Eversons get here at eight.

And felt as though he'd been given a reprieve from the death sentence, a chance to appeal, when he got out of the shower and saw her response.

Can we do 7:30? I have some emails to answer.

Business as usual.
Thank God.
They were going to pretend that nothing had happened.
And if he was lucky, the alcohol-induced insanity that had come over him in the wee hours of the morning would fade and dissipate until he completely forgot that he'd ever had the most exquisite pleasure of being in between Megan Latimer's legs.

Sober, capable, dressed in blue pants, matching tailored jacket and cream-colored blouse, Megan refused to give credence to the knot in her stomach as she rode the elevator down to the hotel's restaurant for the meet with Danny prior to their scheduled breakfast with their new client. The fingers she ran through her hair might have mucked it up, but the short tousled blonde style she'd been wearing since college didn't tell on her.

She could do the job. No doubts there. Was ready and eager to help.

But could she and Danny save their friendship?

The thought brought another pang. Another bout of panic.

Never, ever, ever had she thought she'd screw up the friendship that was her rock. Danny was the one constant in her life that she trusted completely. Even more than she trusted her parents.

One completely stupid, alcohol-induced mistake wasn't going to end her world as she knew it, was it?

Or would it implode a relationship that had been built with more than a decade of meaningful contributions?

If she and Danny were teenagers, she'd have a slew of answers to that question.

Ask her about a child's relationship capabilities, norms, needs, and she was on it. Had written published papers on the topics that had gained national acclaim.

But adults?

She and Danny weren't kids. And, clearly, though of course she'd studied them in school, adult relationships weren't her thing.

The elevator dinged. The door opened to the lobby. Time for breakfast—with her client. And Danny.

She pushed the eleventh floor because it was closest to her finger.

Headed back up.

She needed time to research. To update herself on theory and read current case studies.

Right. That was it. She needed time.

Who was she kidding?

If she and Danny could just pretend those blurry moments of ecstasy hadn't happened, then she could get this all figured out.

Formulate the necessary plan to get them back on track and keep them there.

Implement it.

I owe him a huge apology.

But she couldn't very well do that. How did you apologize for something that you were pretending never happened?

You didn't.

So as uncomfortable as it made her, as much as she hated going against her normal course of behavior, she had to follow the path she'd just chosen. She'd made the mess and until she had a cleanup plan, she was going to have to live with the discomfort.

Assuming Danny had telepathically picked up on her decision to pretend that the most incredible hour of her life had never happened…or, better yet, shared her point of view.

About pretending, not about the sex. She knew better than that. She'd been friends with him long enough to hear all about his exploits—from some of her friends, too. Danny excelled in physical pleasure, so it was absolutely no surprise to find that he knew how to give her pleasure on a level she hadn't even known existed.

But that didn't matter. Because the facts that had kept them friends for so many years were the same. He was kind, genuine, caring. Her best friend.

The door opened again on the eleventh floor to another empty hall—as if the fates were well aware that she shouldn't be facing another human being. She pushed the lobby button. Started back down.

She knew that Danny liked women, in the plural. He always had.

Megan was a love-of-your-life—though she hadn't found it yet—one-man-for-the-rest-of-her-life kind of woman, who was only going to be happy with a one-woman kind of man. She had trust issues.

And she trusted Danny with her life. Her heart.

But she did not trust him to be faithful to her body. Wouldn't even ask it of him. What kind of friend would she be if she started to want her best bud to be someone he was not? If she hoped he'd become someone he wouldn't be happy being?

The thought remained. Solid and sure. Taking her all the way back down to the ground floor. Propelling her out of the elevator, around the corner and through a throng of people to the arched entryway of the restaurant.

And nearly ran into Danny who stepped away from a wall as she walked in.

"Thirty seconds more and you'd have been late, Latimer," he said. "You almost owed me fifty bucks."

"In your dreams, Danny Boy." She grinned at the nickname he playfully hated, though her face felt like it was cracking with the effort.

"Admit it, you were almost late."

"Almost only counts in horseshoes and hand grenades. And you think I'm going to blow a six-year record?" In the past, she'd been known to try to cram too many things into a minute and had ended up late often enough to get a reputation for it.

But she'd hated the reputation.

Had taken accountability and changed her actions. Just between her and Danny, the accountability had become a fine, a fifty-dollar bill, any time she was a minute or more late.

And, really, Danny didn't need know that it was only by luck that she'd made it to their meeting point with thirty seconds to spare. Or rather, fate had. If the elevator had made even one stop during her sojourn, she'd have blown a six-year victory over self.

And, at that moment, she couldn't have cared less. She'd have gladly handed over five hundred dollars, five thousand dollars, to have him greet her in the completely normal fashion he just had.

Last night, they may have gone dangerously off course, but the strength of their friendship had sustained them—allowing them to get back on course relatively unscathed.

Because it was what they both wanted and needed.

She'd have given every dime she had for that gift.

"Sammie's a great kid." Joe Everson looked Danny in the eye as he spoke, his arm around the back of the booth behind his wife.

Breakfast, small talk and an alarming awareness of the beautiful woman beside him had come and gone. On his third cup of coffee, Danny was fully focused, as was his partner. He loved working with Dr. Megan Latimer. Her professionalism, her intuitiveness and intelligence gave him full confidence, every time.

And she knew how to compartmentalize. As did he.

They'd learned from each other.

"She's got a mind of her own," Lindy told them. "We don't want you to think she's easily manipulated, because she's not. Which is what's making this so incredibly difficult…" The woman's voice cracked, and her husband took over.

"We taught Sammie to have confidence in her thoughts, to express them."

"…and to listen to her heart," Lindy said, her lips firm again as she visibly gathered her composure. "Mind and heart…she knows it takes both to make good decisions for a happy life."

Meg nodded. Danny felt the brush of her suit

jacket against his. Didn't take the usual comfort from the contact. Instead, he felt an electric current, which was not good.

It passed swiftly, though, which gave him hope.

The well-to-do couple went on to describe how their daughter, Samantha, who'd lived in Blaine, on their dairy farm her entire life had met a boy, Carter, at a school track meet. Carter lived with his mother, Bella, about half an hour from Blaine, Wisconsin, in a little berg known for its fishing.

Bella worked as a waitress at a truck stop out by the freeway, and during summer months, when their little town of Mandel was alive with fisherman, Carter worked down at the marina, scooping bait, among other things.

Joe talked about how he'd liked Carter so much at first. The teen didn't drink or do drugs, would bring Sammie home a few minutes before curfew every time they were together. Carter had looked him in the eye when he spoke with him and didn't seem to be in any hurry to get away, would hang around and talk. Joe appreciated how Carter could make Sammie laugh.

"And then things changed," Lindy interjected. "Sammie started getting this tone of voice when she talked to us, like she was irritated with us. At first, I thought she was just going through that stage where kids think they're smarter than their parents or something, though it was coming on later than I'd heard it would. But it was more than that. She resented anything I told her, like I didn't have a right to tell her anything because what did I know... I lived a blessed life. I didn't know what it was to suffer, or be in need..."

Lindy's voice faded as her chin started to tremble. Megan sat stoically beside him, but Danny knew, if he glanced her way, he'd see compassion in her gaze.

He didn't glance. Didn't trust himself not to get distracted by something that absolutely did not belong at that table.

Or in any business meeting.

"I came down a little hard on her on that one," Joe said, picking up for his wife, frowning, his tone contrite. "Lindy had it rougher than most growing up, with an alcoholic father who never kept a job. Her mom died when she was just a kid, and she was basically raised by her older brother and sister. Those kids made a family, but they went through hell to stay together and keep the two-room shack their father rented, keep the heat on, and keep food on the table. Sammie knew some of it, but clearly not enough, and I kind of blasted her with that information."

"How'd that go?" Megan spoke up beside him, drawing Danny's gaze, and filling him with admiration, too, as he saw her intent look and knew that her brain was in full working gear.

Joe's shrug wasn't encouraging. "She started to cry, to apologize. Seemed to really be coming around..."

"I saw a look in her eyes when she came over

to hug me that I hadn't seen in a while…" Lindy stopped, and then, in almost a professional tone, as though that was the only way she could get through it, she started in again. "But the next time she was out with Carter, she came home with that same attitude and resentment…"

Joe tapped the table, letting Danny see the pain inside. "She made a snide comment about being in five minutes before curfew and went straight up to her room and shut the door. And locked it." He paused and then, with a sigh, said, "We've never given her a reason to lock her door against us."

"It felt more symbolic than anything," Lindy said with more strength. "After that, we found out that she'd been stealing from us. I got a call from a gallery here in Milwaukee about a gilded pen I'd bought Joe being brought in for sale. The pen is old and registered and Samantha was young to be a collector and the gallery owner figured he better check it out. We didn't press charges, just let the sale go through, but we confronted Samantha and she admitted that she'd taken it. She said it was a pen Joe rarely used just sitting around when the money could be spent for new clothes and a set of silverware that matched and didn't have dings in it that caught at your lip when you ate."

Danny was about ready to start into his spiel, explaining first about the Sierra's Web firm of experts and how they worked—and billed—when Joe glanced at Lindy and then, with obvious distress, she said, "Then last week Sammie came home while Joe was at the dairy and told me she was pregnant and was going to be moving in with Carter and his mother."

Lindy paused, then said, "She threw things into her backpack and walked out. I followed her, but Carter was waiting in his mother's car at the end of the drive. I'd already called Joe, and he pulled in two minutes after they'd left."

Tears filled Lindy's eyes. The woman sniffed. Blinked. And lost her composure to the emotion consuming her.

And Danny's whole case turned sideways. Pregnancy didn't change the legalities. Not in Wisconsin, while Samantha was still underage. But it brought in a whole slew of addendums to what he'd thought was going to be a fairly straight shot for him.

None of which included the further emotional strain on all involved.

"I called the police as soon as I got home." Joe took up the narrative for his wife. "They went to Carter's and brought Sammie home, since she's a minor, but the next day, she left again. From everything she's spewing, it's very clear that Carter and Bella have gotten ahold of her thoughts. Manipulation 101."

Meg didn't move, but Danny knew she'd be making strong mental notes. For Samantha's sake.

"We could have kept calling the police to bring her home," Lindy said with a heavy breath. "We were told to get a restraining order out against Carter and his mother, too, but if we do either of those things, we're just going to push her further away, and then she'll be far less likely to come to us when she needs help. She's our baby. And she's pregnant. She's going to need medical care and…" The dark-haired woman, looking like she hadn't slept in weeks, dug in her purse and came up with a tissue as the tears started again.

"I did some research and found Sierra's Web," Joe said then. "I made a couple of calls to some people I know who knew someone…you guys did some work for the governor a few years back. Anyway, you come highly recommended, and so here we are. We want our daughter back. And we want her to want to come back. To be mentally healthy again, and move back home of her own free will. We also realize that's a tall order."

Danny nodded, glanced at Meg, and when their gazes met, the silent conversation seemed as well understood as if they'd been speaking aloud. And was strictly professional. It was how they rolled.

And what made them so good together.

Tilted his head in silent question. *Was she on board to take the case with him?*

Megan nodded, meeting his glance full-on.

And he breathed his first easy breath since awaking in utter horror early that morning.

Chapter Four

They'd done it. They'd crossed the hurdle separating them from their right path. Were back on the road they'd been building their entire adult lives.

Megan allowed herself a bit of giddiness, teamed with a load of relief as she sat next to her business partner, noting that the usually impeccable knot of the tie at his neck during working hours was actually somewhat askew.

And then her focus was completely back on the conversation at hand. On the aching parents who might or might not get their hearts' desires.

"Before we have you sign the Sierra's Web paperwork, I need to make our roles here clear," Danny told the Eversons, something she'd heard him say many times before, sounding exactly as he had any other time.

Another wave of relief swept over her. They really were good.

"I work for you," he told the couple. "I am solely here to try to get you what you want, through legal means. I'll advise you on all of your rights and means in which to achieve them. If you tell me to proceed, I proceed. Period."

Both sets of forty-year-old eyes were wide open and pinned on him. Lindy, mouth slightly agape, looked as though she'd been saved from hell. Megan wanted to tell her it hadn't happened yet.

That it might not happen.

And she would. As soon as they were officially hired and she had her first session with them.

And while she'd seen dashed hopes too many times, she also knew the vital importance of having hope.

"And Dr. Latimer will be working solely for your daughter's well-being." Danny delivered the line that was of critical importance. "You're paying her to work with Samantha, to counsel her, and, if it comes to that, to give expert testimony to the court on Samantha's behalf. So, while you are hiring her, she's not here to make your daughter do what you want her to do. She's here to give her professional advice on what's best for your daughter."

Joe and Lindy nodded in unison. Quite emphatically.

"You need to understand—" Megan leaned in to speak softly, as her next words were critical "—if, in my opinion, Samantha is of sound and healthy mind and would be better served living with Carter, that is the opinion I must give the court. And as I counsel her, if that does turn out to be my opinion, I will counsel her accordingly, on how best to achieve the goals that she believes are right for her."

Lindy frowned. Joe sat back. Crossed his arms. Assessed her.

Megan didn't budge.

Danny didn't either.

"We love Sammie," Lindy said slowly, glanced at Joe, who looked back at her. "We want what's best for her."

Joe's nod was firm. Chin jutting, he looked back at Megan, and said, "We understand."

"So, I have your cooperation in a full and honest assessment and counsel—if Samantha is open to it?"

"You'll keep us apprised, right?" Lindy asked. "Even if what you have to tell us isn't what we want to hear."

"Absolutely. And in full disclosure, Samantha will know that as her parents, you have the right to be privy to the information. Technically, as she is underage, you have the right to be in the room for every session, but I'm going to advise against that one for now. We're dealing with a teenager who is already feeling resentful, and I believe that forcing sessions with me with you present will only exacerbate the situation. It also will undermine her trust in me as an impartial professional who's on her side. Instead, she'll see us as a pack of adults who only want to keep her from doing what she thinks she most wants and needs. She'll build defenses against me from the get-go, and our chances of reaching our goal will be less attainable. But she'll be given a choice to have one or both of you present, and if she prefers that, you will be in the room with her for every session."

"She won't choose that," Lindy said, her eyes getting moist again. Her lip quivered. She took a deep breath, and then looked straight at Megan, connecting with something inside her that wasn't usually at the worktable...a sense of kinship. Which made no sense whatsoever.

And raised a defensive shield within Megan. Something to analyze as soon as she was alone.

"Until six months ago, Sammie was my best friend," Lindy said shakily, unknowingly pushing Megan's baggage back where it belonged. "From the time she was born, we were joined at the hip. And then suddenly...she doesn't like me? I have no idea what I've done. I spend every waking hour trying to figure it out. I come up with things...you know, was I too much in her life? Should I not have gone to every track meet or been involved with every concession stand? I was trying to share her life with her, but maybe I inserted myself too much…"

Megan's heart ached. For Lindy. And for Samantha, too.

"I can't answer any of that just yet," she said. "But what I can promise you is that I will do my best to figure it out. And, if things go well, maybe we can set up a session with you and Sammie together, where we can talk through some of this." It was the best she could do.

And for the moment, it was enough. The Eversons nodded again. They signed the paperwork—after insisting on paying for breakfast—and left Danny and Megan in the hotel lobby with warm handshakes, profuse thanks and…time alone.

Megan wasn't ready for that.

She nearly wept with relief when Danny immediately excused himself to return a couple of calls that apparently had just come in, judging by his frown as he scrolled on his phone.

She needed a moment to align herself.

That moment with Lindy…a kinship? Like, what, mother to mother? No. She couldn't go there. Would be borrowing trouble. Worrying before she had any cause to worry. Logically, she knew all of that.

She also knew that she'd never, ever, not even once in her life, had unprotected sex.

Until last night with Danny.

She knew he'd assumed she was on the pill. He

knew she'd gone on it when she and Kurt had moved in together. She'd shared with Danny that her mom had been on it for years and had then had trouble conceiving, not that the two were necessarily related. She'd just needed to work it through. If she went on the pill would she be lessening her chances of having children of her own?

Danny had listened. Hadn't said much.

She'd talked herself down from her worry ledge, had gone on the pill, and that had been that.

But Danny didn't know that she'd been having some issues with headaches and had chosen, especially considering the recent breakup, to give her body a break from that known side effect. Just hadn't been worth talking about it on their weekly call.

Oh, God, what had she done?

Calculations ran through her head as she waited for Danny to finish his calls and meet her back in the lobby for the drive out to Blaine.

She hadn't had a period in a couple of weeks.

Her cycle hadn't been regular since she'd gone off the pill.

She could be ovulating. Danny's sperm could be fertilizing.

She could take a morning-after pill.

Her heart dismissed that idea. Immediately. So there was nothing more for her to do with the issue except get a better handle on her thought process by working harder to keep her mind on healthy things, real things.

And get on with the life she'd made for herself.

In a couple of weeks, if there was anything more to consider, she'd do so at that time.

Until then, she had a pregnant teenager who needed help.

A business partner who was counting on her to remain professional.

And...a friendship to salvage.

Shoulders squared, satchel hanging from the right one as always, Megan was ready to go when Danny approached a few minutes later.

She smiled at him.

He smiled back.

And out of the blue, for no explicable reason, she wished she had time to call her mom for relationship advice.

Something she hadn't sought from either of her parents since they'd told her they were divorcing.

On the way to Blaine, while Danny drove, and fretted some, Megan called Samantha, who'd already heard from her parents regarding the psychiatrist they'd hired on her behalf. She was able to set up a meeting for her and Danny with the teen at a coffee shop in Blaine, not far from the high school she attended.

If they had a perfect world moment, Samantha

would realize the seriousness of her situation when she heard from Danny that the law forced her home. Ideally, she'd willingly agree to live with her parents until she turned eighteen.

He and Megan could then be on separate planes out of Milwaukee that night and catch up later in the week.

Ideally.

After he'd had time to get in some serious workouts, go on a date or two, get involved in an intense, long-term case, he'd figure out how to assure Megan that he had no intention of touching her body ever again so that he didn't lose her friendship.

To wipe his body's memory of the best sex he'd ever had…

"She's borrowing Carter's mother's car to come meet us and has already warned me that we're wasting our time," Megan said, after hanging up from the call she'd just made to inform Lindy and Joe Everson of the upcoming appointment. Samantha had adamantly refused to have them there, just as Lindy had predicted.

"So, you take the lead." It was a given when they were dealing with antagonistic custodial issues. And with a baby involved…

"At least until we see if I can get her to talk to me. Her dad might be right that she'll respond to logic and legal pressure, at least long enough to get her home."

Then it was up to Megan to do what she could to keep Samantha there without her parents having to take their child to court.

The hope was that his job would be to provide legal facts, and just a bit of pressure, to get the child home without a single motion being filed.

"Given the very little bit you have to go on—her tone of voice was even, coupled with the fact that she agreed to meet with us right away—what do you think my chances are of getting her home tonight?"

She couldn't possibly know, but he'd learned that her initial judgments were right 80 percent of the time.

Megan, staring out the side window, hadn't answered.

Because she didn't have good news to offer?

Or because she was off in another world and hadn't heard his question?

He could hope, if she was daydreaming, or nightmaring, that her mind was on a beach in The Bahamas.

"Megan?"

"Yeah?"

"This isn't going to go smoothly, is it?" The case was all he was referring to. Just the case.

"Probably not." Was she just referring to the case? Or to them?

Was he really going to turn into some dude who nitpicked relationship stuff? When had he ever wallowed in…anything? He questioned. He discovered. He chose. He moved on.

And couldn't for the life of him come up with anything to say to lighten the moment. Or bring them back to "them." What would he be talking about if he hadn't slept with his best friend the night before?

He couldn't talk about what they'd done, couldn't make it a "thing" by actually acknowledging it.

But he also couldn't stick just to business when they were alone. Their time together was precious, and they generally filled up every second of it with conversation about everything under the sun. There'd be something wrong for sure if they only talked business.

"You hear anything about the wedding?"

"I had texts from Jeanine and Shelly this morning," she told him, glancing his way. And then spent the next several minutes regaling him with the things her friends had said, what they hadn't said, the compassion they'd shown her, which she'd hated because it made her feel like she was to be pitied. It was like she'd just been sitting there waiting for that door to be opened.

"Did you let them know that you were relieved that it wasn't you?" he asked, chancing a glance at her, shooting over a signature grin, and was rewarded with a genuine smile.

"Of course not," she said, as his gaze quickly returned to the road. "I told them both that I hoped Kurt and his new wife were very happy together."

"And then you said you were glad it wasn't you, right?" He knew she wouldn't have. It wasn't her way.

But he liked her smile. Liked that he could still make her smile.

"And then I said that I was almost late for my meeting with you and wasn't going to give you the satisfaction of winning fifty dollars."

"They know about our bet?" Why the idea pleased him, he didn't know. And didn't want to ask. Another conundrum. He'd never had to watch his thoughts around Meg before.

Maybe he should have done.

And...just before she'd come down that morning, she'd been thinking about their bet? Not about the sex they'd had? A good sign.

A very good sign.

As was the one that said Blaine was two miles ahead.

They'd worked together for the first time after their one-night stand, had been able to talk like friends, and no one was drowning.

At least he hoped they weren't.

For him, it was a bit of a touch and go thing.

But that would pass. Another few hours, a day at the most, and he'd have his sea legs firmly beneath him.

Chapter Five

"My parents just don't understand." It wasn't the first time Megan had heard the comment from a client in session. Wasn't even the hundredth. She saw Danny's glance through peripheral vision, knew he'd just had the same thought, and continued to focus on her seventeen-year-old client. Danny was working for Joe and Lindy Everson, while she was Samantha's only voice in the adult world that would be deciding her fate.

"I love Carter and he loves me. Neither of us wanted to get pregnant, yet. No way my parents were going to let me go on the pill. They'd have stopped me from seeing Carter if they knew we were having sex. We were using birth control, but..." The young woman shrugged, but didn't look away. "I know we're young, he knows we're young. Our road isn't going to be easy. But Bella, his mother, is helping us figure things out. She had Carter when she was young, too, but his dad skated on her, and she's managed to provide for them by herself. We'll have both of us, and Bella's help, too, and we only have to make it until I'm twenty-one and come into my inheritance from my grandparents. The baby won't even be four yet…"

And *bing*. Her senses buzzed. She could tell from Danny's jiggling knee that he was getting tenser.

And while for the first time that touch sent a bit of a shock through her, too, she quickly dismissed the awareness in lieu of the job at hand.

Joe and Lindy Everson hadn't mentioned the trust fund. They'd have known about it, but had left Megan and Danny to do their jobs. To find out any relevant or pertinent information through Samantha or during paid legal sessions.

The distraught parents hadn't used the morning's meeting to prejudice them.

Megan's respect for the Eversons grew.

As did her dread for them in the coming days.

She had no doubt they'd get Samantha home, probably until her eighteenth birthday. But during the battle, the teen could try to show cause that her parents were unfit. She hoped to God it didn't go that far.

And knew that it could…

"Bella has said that Carter and I can stay with her until we graduate. I'm going to take care of things at the house for her and Carter is working at the diner evenings and weekends, washing dishes..."

Samantha, very clearly, had come to the meeting armed and with one goal in mind. To get her parents off her back.

She'd come well-armed.

With a plan she couldn't have concocted on her own.

And one that hadn't just been put in place since that morning. Unless Carter had just been offered the job that day...

"How long has Carter been working at the diner?" Nothing they'd been given had stated anything about the teenager having any job other than a summer marina job.

"He starts tonight."

She nodded. Schooled her expression to remain open. Encouraging. Because her heart felt for the girl, and because her mind told her Samantha Everson might very well need her help far more than she knew.

Megan would put her own worries, her mistakes and consequences completely aside because her life's work was her job, and her clients deserved her best.

Because she cared that much...

She tapped Danny's knee quickly. Twice. Glad that he was there. For more reasons than one. He knew of the mistake that was weighing heavily on her that day.

And was helping her rectify it by being the best friend he'd always been.

"You are aware that, legally, Bella Wilson has no right to have you living in her home, aren't you?" Danny said on cue. The two-tap meant it was his turn.

Good. Talk about Bella's rights. Not the Eversons. Or even Samantha's.

That small level of distance could make a difference. As Danny would know.

"She doesn't care if she gets in trouble." Samantha's immediate reply wasn't encouraging. "She's not afraid, and she'll say that to anyone..." The young blue-eyed, blonde mother-to-be sent a steely look to both of them, back and forth, as though she could inject them with the fact that her way was right, and she was going to have it.

Megan admired her grit. Had she, Megan, ever been that certain about anything in her life?

Maybe before college, but she didn't remember it that way. Certainly not in the last several years.

"Do you care if she gets in trouble?" Danny's next words landed, and Megan was reminded why she relied on him so strongly in a professional sense.

She had a momentary sense of relief that they were still in their groove, but quickly focused on Samantha. Her immediate stiffening, the straightening and then, slow rounding of her shoulders. The way she blinked a few times, and then frowned.

More anger, more bravado would be coming, she was sure of that, but she also took heart. Lindy and Joe Everson had raised a daughter with a conscience.

From there, a good outcome could grow.

And Danny, obviously sensing as much, leaned in for his best shot at getting the girl home with her parents.

"She could be arrested, lose her job. She and Carter could be evicted from their home for non-payment of rent if that happens. And with charges on her record, she could have trouble getting another job," he said.

He wasn't arguing the bigger points, dealing with any of the real issues in terms of Samantha's mental health, well-being or happiness, but that wasn't his job. He was doing what he did best, getting the child to safety first and foremost, and doing it as kindly as he possibly could. Sitting there, hearing the compassion in his tone as he laid out what was likely to happen if things didn't de-escalate, Megan was reminded of how very much his friendship meant to her.

"The law doesn't bend for falling in love, or even for accidental pregnancy, Samantha, and, in this case, the law is clear-cut. Your parents are legally responsible for you. The law requires that they keep you at home until you're eighteen."

"They could let me go, if they wanted to."

His half nod of acknowledgment toned down the defensive set of Samantha's upper body language. "But only if they're honestly convinced that living outside their home is in your best interest."

When Samantha said nothing, he continued. "Have you done anything to help them see that it might be in your best interest to stay with Bella and Carter Wilson?"

The teenager, looking ready to cry, instead of raging for battle, shook her head and the knot in Megan's stomach started to ease.

"Perhaps if you could agree to come home, even if just for a short time, to be open-minded and have a conversation with them, expectant mother to parent, you and Carter could have the future you're building without anyone getting hurt..."

"I don't know... I..."

"Maybe you start with some kind of written agreement between the three of you. Something I could draw up, even, that states the boundaries of behavior, the expectations and goals that all three of you agree to..."

"You actually think my parents would sign such a thing?" Clear disdain rode with the words as the look in the girl's eyes hardened.

"I know they would," Danny said with the confidence Megan had known he had. "I already have their word that they will do so." Samantha's eyes grew moist before her gaze dropped.

"They love you, Samantha. And just as I'm certain you'll do for your child, your parents want what's best for you." Danny's tone, his word choice were as good as anything Megan could have offered herself.

And it was in everyone's best interest if she remained silent, letting him handle the Eversons' business so she could hopefully begin building trust within Samantha that Megan was there for her, not her parents.

"I..." The young blue eyes glanced Megan's way, and then back at Danny, as Samantha's features took on a youth and a new beauty with their softening. "I guess I..."

Her phone, which she'd had in hand the entire time they'd been talking dinged. Samantha jumped, glanced at the screen, as did Megan.

Carter's name flashed with a text message Megan couldn't fully decipher upside down.

But she made out enough. don't let.

"No," Samantha said, glancing back up, and Megan's heart dropped. "You aren't going to manipulate me into doing what they want..."

Carter, or his mother, had gotten to her. Reminded her.

They hadn't trusted her to remain strong during an interview on her own. And so, they'd interrupted, rather than waiting for Samantha to contact them at meeting's end. Most likely.

A classic sign of manipulation.

If she'd needed proof that her client was a victim, as her parents had claimed, she'd just had it. Whether or not the Wilsons were after Everson wealth, was yet to be determined.

"Believe me," Samantha was saying, her gaze hard again. "They might have you believing they'd be open-minded, but they won't be. I've lived with them, you haven't. They're so used to their entitlement, to thinking that they can have things their way, that they can't open their minds to other ways that might be equally, or even more, for the best. I love Carter, who most definitely isn't from the crowd of kids my parents want me to hang with. And I'm pregnant. I don't fit their pretty life. And I don't want to live in a world where I have to pretend. Not anymore."

When Megan and Danny bumped knees simultaneously, Megan said, "Okay. Fair enough. You don't want to enter into an amicable agreement, that's fair." And then she looked at Danny. "Mr. Tremaine?"

"So, if you're sure that's your decision—"

"I'm sure," the girl cut him off.

Damn.

The kid was likely cutting off her own best chance without even knowing it.

Sometimes life didn't play fair.

Like when it led one to get drunk and sleep with one's woman-magnet best friend?

Shaking off the thought, she listened as Danny

outlined next steps, from a legal standpoint. Heard him talk about her status as expert witness psychiatrist and what that entailed, about court orders for her return home, and the possibility of a restraining order against Carter and Bella that could be issued, temporarily, as early as that night or the next morning...

And then she interrupted. "Let's at least try to keep that one off the table for now," she said. And Danny, bless, him, though it wasn't usual for her to interrupt at that point, sat back and let her speak. "I'd like to try to see if we can, just for now, get a few days for you and me to talk, for me to meet Carter and Bella, if they're willing, before we immediately go for the jugular."

When Samantha looked at Danny, he looked from her to Megan and back again, saying nothing.

"If your parents are willing to sit tight for a couple of days, at least in terms of calling the police to bring you home again, or filing for a restraining order, would you be willing to meet with me? And to be open and honest with me when we do meet?"

"And my parents won't file anything with the court to make me move home?" Samantha's tone had changed again, grown softer, as she looked at Danny.

"I can't guarantee that," he said. "As a matter of fact, I can't, in good conscience, even advise it..." The girl's expression hardened, and he quickly added, "But...with no evidence of immediate physical harm, the motion will likely take a few days to work its way through the system…whereas a call to police, or the filing of an emergency restraining order, could have immediate effect…"

"Fine," Samantha said, able to see the obvious choice. "But if you think my meeting with you—" she looked at Megan "—is going to change anything, you're going to be disappointed."

Maybe.

Megan prayed that, at some point, Samantha would see that they both wanted to help her. That her parents did, too.

But in lieu of that, she'd take the small victory the girl had just unknowingly handed herself.

Danny had always admired the hell out of Meg's professional skills, her constant calm, her ability to read people and to clue him in without saying a word.

He'd never, ever, even a little bit, been turned on by looking back over a meeting and recognizing everything she'd done right. Done to help a teenager she'd never met until that day.

He'd known her goal going in…to try to establish the beginning of a sense of trust between her and Samantha. He'd even known largely how she'd go about reaching that goal.

He'd seen it dozens of times.

He'd never had the hots for her, walking out of a meeting.

God, commit him to hell, right then and there. By

what cruel twist of fate was his libido suddenly turning traitor on him? Sabotaging the one relationship he valued above all others.

It sure as hell didn't take any kind of expert to see that a man who liked the company of women, and a woman who needed monogamous permanency, didn't fit.

He knew better than most how fleeting sexual attraction really was. And how much damage it could cause to relationships when it went cold. No way was he letting physical desire burn up what he'd built with Megan.

No. Way.

He'd flee the country first.

But before that he had to help the Everson family find peace.

After a quick call to Kelly Chase, one of the seven Sierra's Web full partners, he waited as Meg walked Samantha out to her car, giving the two of them time for private conversation to set up the best times and places to meet. He experienced another sharp, knee-jerking bolt of physical reaction as he saw her come back through the door to join him. The way she'd had her gaze trained in his direction, as though seeing him there meant something...

It had *always* meant something. The pleasure that crossed Meg's face when they saw each other had always been something he'd noticed.

But never sexually.

Maybe he needed to see someone. Make sure there wasn't something weird going on, a surge of testosterone in his system, glands out of whack, or something.

She was the one with the medical degree, but he most definitely wasn't asking *her*.

"It's not going to be pretty," she said as she sat down across from him this time. A move of which he fully approved.

"Or easy," he guessed. On so many fronts. "I'd like you to come with me to see the Eversons. I've already called Kelly to let her know we'll need her services, but I think they'll feel better hearing about Samantha's reactions and behaviors today from you."

Her nod was calm. Normal. He was thankful.

She ran her fingers through the short-cropped blond hair that he used to tease her about. Calling her bed head. Wondering if she'd stuck her finger in a light socket. Telling her she'd forgotten to do her hair. He hadn't meant any of it. She'd never taken him seriously, either.

How in the hell had he ever thought that tousled look anything but a total turn on? The woman oozed sexuality. How could he have missed that for so many years?

"I'm glad Kelly's on her way. Did she say how soon she thought she could get here?" Did Meg sound relieved?

"She's going to try for tomorrow. She'll take a

cab to the hotel and rent a second car from there if we need one."

While Kelly, also a renowned psychiatrist, was Meg's team leader at the firm, the Sierra's Web partner would be working as Danny's expert witness in Blaine—interviewing Lindy and Joe Everson and advising the court as to her opinion of their fitness as parents. Thankfully, there were no police reports, no record of any kind of domestic disturbance within the Everson home, or in Samantha's personal history, so he'd be speaking with school personnel, the track coach, Samantha's teachers, parents of Samantha's friends, people in town who knew Lindy and Joe, volunteered with them, worked with and for them, to gather as much evidence as he could to show the judge that Samantha was being raised by responsible, loving, healthy parents. And knew from experience that Kelly's testimony would weigh more with the judge than any of the rest of it. Though, if he could get the governor to vouch for them, that might help, too. He added the state's top man to his mental list of calls to make.

"And this gives you three, maybe four days at the most, before we move to restrain Carter and Bella Wilson from having contact with Samantha." It wasn't enough time. He wished he could give her more.

"I know. Hope to God, I can reach her before then."

"You think they're right, don't you? Lindy and Joe. Their daughter is being manipulated."

"I think that she's got some very definite thought processes going on in her head. And that she's fighting some natural reactions, and instincts, to remain true to them."

"She's being programmed."

"Yes, but by who, or what, and for what purpose, I don't yet know. Her love for Carter seems genuine, not fear-based. But she loves her parents, too. I'd bet my life on it."

The response wasn't a surprise. His huge rush of emotion for the woman who emitted it knocked him upside the head. Meg was one of a kind. A treasure.

Her unique ability to see what others missed, to assess when the answers seemed clear to him, to find what no one knew was there, was a gift.

There was no one, absolutely no one, he'd rather have working with him.

Or have for a trusted confidant.

Somehow, he had to get through his sudden other attractions to her and forget he'd ever felt her body holding his.

There simply was no other option.

Chapter Six

The meeting with Joe and Lindy Everson went pretty much as Megan would have scripted it. Lindy cried more than she had in the public restaurant. Joe exhibited marked up levels of frustration. All reactions within a normal range to the situation. Both were panicked.

Neither was happy about waiting a few days before sending the police after their daughter for a second time.

But both were committed to doing so.

Despite that respite, Megan knew that emotions running too high for too long could create domestic disaster. The young couple could run away. Joe could call the police in spite of the agreement he'd just made not to do so. The Eversons could drive to the modest Wilson home and create havoc.

Bottom line was that Danny, Kelly and Megan had to be at the top of their games and incredibly fast, if they were going to save the current family and potential future one.

A baby was on the way. For Megan, that changed everything.

Legally, not so much. After all, Samantha was underaged, under her parents' care, and until the child was born, her care included the pregnant state of her body.

But emotionally, Samantha would be much harder for Megan to reach. Not only did she have the teen's obvious love, devotion and loyalty to Carter to contend with, but she had a mama's instinctive need to provide for her unborn child. And loyalty to her newly forming family.

Not to mention the surge of hormones that often rendered pregnant women less capable of keeping their emotions on an even keel.

Which could hinder rationality. Most particularly in an already hormonal teen.

"The fact that the Eversons are making medical care easily accessible to their daughter, without forcing her to come home to get their help with co-pays, speaks to their sincerity," she said aloud as they left the huge and lovely ranch property where Samantha had grown up.

"Their insurance covers prenatal care, but not the delivery—and not the child after delivery," Danny said, pointing out what they both knew.

But something they weren't sure Samantha—or Carter—fully understood. The Eversons' insurance policy didn't cover a baby. But the prenatal care was included because it covered Samantha's body.

Something Megan was going to have to press home to the teenage mother-to-be.

"She'll likely qualify for government assistance for the child," Danny said, filling the silence when Megan failed to respond as usual to his former statement.

She wanted to apologize. For her silence, and for the night before. But she couldn't risk allowing the unsaid between them to explode in the middle of a critical job.

How could she hope to successfully communicate with him about something she didn't understand? Something she couldn't even process for herself?

"Her whole life is about to change so drastically, and I'm not sure she comprehends that at all," Megan said aloud.

How could a few minutes, one reckless, careless activity, change an entire lifetime forevermore?

And how could a child have the ability to cope with that when a grown adult was unable to comprehend even a distant possibility of facing such a thing?

"You want to stop on the way back to get something to eat?"

"That sounds great." She blurted a couple of choices she'd seen on the way in, eager to pull her mind up to the moment's reality. And grasping at the opportunity to avoid awkward moments in the hotel when they got back.

A lack of trust had been forged by a stupid, alcohol-induced mistake because she'd been feeling uncharacteristically sorry for herself and had come on to him. She hated that.

Her solution: pick up something on the way or order room service—separately—and pretend they'd eaten alone before while on the road together.

As it was, they found a Spanish place with high booths, giving them privacy, but cathedral ceilings and open air so that they were surrounded by noise, too. The high energy place had many employees, all clearly trying to give their guests a celebratory feel, while also providing personal privacy.

Any other time she'd have absolutely adored the place. And sharing the experience with him.

They analyzed the menu together—as always. Choosing to order, and share, two different entrées, and a plantain appetizer, too.

When the wine waiter stopped at their table, she quickly shook her head. Sparkling water was fine for her.

Danny ordered tea. As he always did when he was

driving at night. In the morning it was coffee with sweet creamer. That hadn't changed since college.

She found the sameness comforting and started to relax.

They talked about the case, as was normal when they were on the road. Kelly would be arriving first thing in the morning, and after dropping her off with the Eversons, Megan would drop Danny at his first appointment—he'd be spending the next day visiting with as many people on his list as he could to firmly establish his clients as completely fit parents—while Megan used the car to make a quick side trip of her own.

She was hoping to see Bella Wilson at work in the morning, a stop-in surprise visit just to observe, before getting back for her session with Samantha.

"It's a tough situation all the way around," she told Danny as they helped themselves to food from each other's plates. "What if Bella is just offering the kids a place to stay because she's a good mom and that's the only way she can help them? What if she's just offering support?"

"How does it support them when it means that Samantha has to defy her parents, have police come after her and be in trouble with the law?"

"What if she's aware that they were a flight risk if she didn't offer them refuge?"

"Then why isn't she talking to Samantha's parents, attempting to share the information with them, working with them to come up with the best solution for their children?"

And there was the rub, of course. Danny wasn't telling her anything she didn't already know. He was playing devil's advocate.

Helping her clarify exactly what she needed to find out.

The time crunch made every second, every query, count.

"It's a question I can pose to Samantha," she said, chewing a last bite of plantain from the appetizer plate they'd set aside. The idea was not to tell the teenager what was going on, but to help her discover truth on her own. To empower her confidence in her own ability to figure things out.

"I grew up like Sammie did," she said, meeting Danny's gaze, telling him something he already knew. "Other than the important difference that the Eversons seem to still love each other. Their relationship seems healthy."

"From everything I've ever heard, your parents' relationship seemed healthy, too. You were the only one who'd seen the change."

"Because it was only visible inside our home," she said slowly, nodding.

"You think one of the Eversons was unfaithful to the other, but they're staying together for Samantha's sake? Until she graduates? Or...were staying together only until then," she said, clarifying. "Now that there's a baby coming…"

She was only speculating.

"The theory makes Kelly's visit that much more critical," Danny said, still eyeing her.

"My folks were still great parents," she said then. "There were no grounds to have ever been able to have them proven unfit."

"I know." He put down his fork, waved off the waiter as he started to approach. "But if you'd fallen in love when you were sixteen, and found yourself unexpectedly pregnant at seventeen…if the father of the baby loved you, too, and wanted to make a family with you…"

She nodded. "The allure would have been incredibly tempting." She sipped from her second bottle of water. Wiped her mouth with her napkin and held on to it. "Definitely could be a powerful motivation," she continued slowly. "Look at me now, thirty-one years old and still hanging on to the hope that I'll one day have the type of family life I shared with my parents when they were happy together. And that, unlike them, I'll be able to make it work till death do us part."

"You've always said that the role of family is critical…"

She had. In fact, she'd told him that most recently when she'd been trying to convince him to think about settling down with a woman he'd been with, exclusively, for a couple of months. She hadn't been insinuating that he should rush out and ask the woman to marry him. Only that he allow himself to consider a different future for himself than he'd once envisioned. He was older, more experienced. His emotional needs were evolving, she'd told him.

And then she'd jumped his bones.

What must he think of her?

Horror-struck, she stared at him. Wondering if he'd read her thoughts accurately—as he so often did.

Or if she'd just followed where Danny's own mind had been going...

"And you pointed out to me that for some, lack of family was a source of freedom that led to joy and internal peace."

They'd left the case behind. She was looking straight at him. Drowning herself with the striking blue color of his eyes, while struggling to stay afloat at the same time.

"Okay, Doc, just say what you have to say and get it over with."

Just like that. The sex they'd had was right there, smack-dab in the middle of the table, exposed and refusing to be swept away like dirty dishes.

A right move on his part. They sure couldn't have it hanging out there when Kelly was sitting with them tomorrow.

"I'm sorry," she said, finding the words a relief,

more than painful. "More than I can say, Danny. I've been sick about this all day, and I hope and pray, I want, more than anything in my life, ever, for us to move past one out-of-character choice and be you and me. I need *us*."

She'd been fighting thoughts all day, refusing to allow them conscious time, and yet, there they all were, out. As hard as she'd tried to stifle them, they'd been battling for release.

"Whoa, wait a minute." His response sank her heart, deep. Making her wish she hadn't eaten. Open-mouthed, she stared at him.

"What's this about you apologizing?"

The words confused her. That part had been a no-brainer. "I took advantage of our friendship, of the fact that I know that you're open to casual sex, to assuage an idiotic sense of not being good enough," she told him. "I didn't even love Kurt. I just let the facts of his rapid wedding get to me, making me obsess over the idea that he'd been unfaithful to me. I was looking for confirmation that I'm desirable," she said, rambling. "And you were safe."

Danny sat back. Assessed her in a way that felt new. And not necessarily good.

"I've really ruined things, haven't I?" The fear had been building all day. The other, thinking about consequences, had only been distraction from what had really been bothering her.

"I don't know how to live without you, Danny." She knew, as the words left her mouth, they were the end. Danny probably needed their friendship as much as she did, but forcing the words, laying the heart open...that was the surest way to get a glimpse of his backside as he raced away.

"You done yet?" The cock of his head, the glint in his eye, were...familiar. Blessedly so.

"Yeah." She held her breath, waiting. Could the great Danny Tremaine really get them out of this mess?

"First, if anyone took advantage, it was me. You were drunk and vulnerable and I was...well...me. But I'm willing to throw out the taking advantage angle if you are."

Watching him, unsure, but willing to remain seated, Megan nodded.

"Second, unless you're going somewhere I can't be, like a nunnery, or to live forever in a woman's restroom, you'd have a hard time losing me. I'm pretty good at getting myself wherever I want or need to be. Assuming where I want to be is mutual to whoever I want or need to be there with."

Flowers started to bloom inside her. She could feel the gentle spreading of their petals in her chest.

"Third..." His gaze sharpened on her, losing any glint of humor. "I value our friendship, too, Meg. Truth be told, ever since I woke up this morning, I've been trying to figure out how to get us back on track."

Her smile came back then. Big and bold. She felt it to her bones. "I think you just did."

"So, we can just agree never to speak of this again?"

"What's to talk about?"

"I'm glad we got that settled."

"Me, too."

They'd put their friendship to the test, a mountainous, life-threatening test, and it had come out on top.

Danny figured he finally understood what a parolee felt like when he'd been set free and given a second chance at being a productive and contributing member of society.

Megan was giving him a second chance.

Giving herself one as well, he'd read into her diatribe.

After a chatty ride home, relief had filled the elevator all the way up to the eleventh floor. He'd waited, as usual, standing at his own door, watching while she got inside hers, and he'd returned the good-night text she'd sent a couple of hours later— their long ago agreed upon communication so neither accidentally woke the other with some work-related issue.

He had a beer in the room as he went over case notes and handled communications for an ongoing case he was involved with in Idaho, and for a potential case in Illinois that he could be called to handle in between filing motions in Blaine and having to argue them before the court. Sierra's Web had lawyers licensed in all fifty states, and many of them, like Danny, had licenses to practice in all UBE states, states with uniform bar exams.

But he had plans to qualify to practice in other states as well. Part of his life plan and a key goal.

One that Megan had found fascinating.

One that would allow them to partner in *any* state on any case that needed her expertise—and a good attorney. She'd have the family she needed, her homelife and he'd be her home away from home. A different kind of home. A friendship that would bond them forever, while still allowing her fidelity to whatever man she married.

He'd seen that as their future…partners forever, in friendship and work.

And was glad to know they were back on track.

Went to sleep with the thought in mind, shortly after she'd texted good night.

And woke the next morning with a hard-on.

He'd spent the night dreaming about her as his partner.

But not a professional one.

The cold shower he took wasn't pleasant, but it worked, for the time being. And as he met Kelly and Meg in the lobby half an hour later, saw Meg's glance, the relief in her eyes when he shot his patented smart aleck smile at her, he figured a lifetime of cold showers, several times a day, would be worth the discomfort to keep his best friend in his life.

A small price to pay, actually.

Chapter Seven

Megan didn't expect to speak with Bella—Carter's mother—that morning. She planned to stop in at the diner, order coffee and be on her way, hoping to catch a glimpse of the woman in her natural habitat. Maybe see her interact with a customer or coworker.

When she walked in, a woman not much older than herself, with plain dark hair pulled back into a ponytail, wearing an old-fashioned pink-and-white diner dress and apron, glanced up and smiled. Watched her order from an older man at the register, and stand waiting.

The woman was still watching when she took her cardboard cup with the white lid and raised it tentatively to her lips. Megan met her gaze over the edge of the cup.

And knew exactly who she was. Bella.

Megan had over an hour before she had to get to Blaine to turn the car back over to Danny.

Coffeepot back on the warmer, Bella Wilson said something to the older man behind the counter and then, wiping her hands on her apron, approached Megan.

"You're the psychiatrist, aren't you?" Her green eyes were assessing, but not accusatory. Or even hesitant in their perusal. Megan's mental note was a positive one. The name badge pinned to the woman's dress confirmed that she was facing Bella Wilson.

"I'm Dr. Latimer," she said kindly, but without a smile. Samantha's future was no laughing matter.

"Sammie described you well," Bella said. "She said she liked your hair."

Megan's nod wasn't meant to be condescending. But she wasn't going to be soft-soled, either. At the same time, she was pleased. The fact that Samantha had carried back something good about her, had had any positive feelings at all during their initial meeting at the coffee shop the day before, was another little piece of hope to hang on to.

Bella nodded toward an empty booth that sat alone in a corner by an old full-size arcade game. Megan, feeling decidedly overdressed in her black pants, off-white cropped jacket with black pockets, and black pumps, followed her.

"She told me that your lawyer friend threatened

me," Bella said as they settled across from each other, her tone calm to match an equally placid expression.

"He's a business partner, Daniel Tremaine, hired by Samantha's parents, and he did not threaten you," Megan quickly pointed out. "He informed Samantha of the legalities she could be facing, which includes your possible arrest. Samantha has a right to know what kind of battle she's waging here. She deserves to know the consequences while she still has time to avoid them. And in fairness to her, she should be aware, ahead of time, of who else she can hurt by her actions because if she cares about you as much as she says she does, she'll suffer later if she knows that you were hurt because of her."

Bella didn't speak right away. Megan had the feeling she'd surprised the other woman.

"I'm here solely for Samantha's benefit," she said, sliding a card out of her jacket pocket and across the table. "I'm a child, adolescent and teen psychiatrist," she continued. "I want to help her."

"She thinks you want to force her to do what her parents want her to do."

"I'm aware of that."

"Then you should also be aware that I would face the possibility of jail before I ever tell a child, a young woman, a friend of my son's that she is not welcome to stay in my home. Would you rather she just ran away? Lived on the streets? I won't push her out. Carter loves her. She's carrying his baby. And there is nothing I won't do for my son. I'm a good mother. Look into me. Look into my son. Check police records, school records, hospital records if you haven't already. We have nothing to hide. And I've faced a lot worse than anything you or the Eversons are going to threaten."

Bella's words could have been a challenge, but they came across so matter-of-fact, Megan believed the woman was speaking her truth.

But had Bella pushed that truth onto Samantha for her own gain?

Or, more likely, Megan was beginning to suspect, for her son's? *There's nothing I won't do for my son.*

The Eversons had given the same impression. There was nothing they wouldn't do for their daughter. Megan's own parents had given her the same sense, might even have told her at some point while she was growing up, that there wasn't anything they wouldn't do for her.

But did that mean breaking the law?

Or manipulating a vulnerable and frightened young woman, coaching her son to do so as well, so that in a few short years he could have a better life than Bella would ever be able to provide for him? Have a chance at a brighter future he might never be able to make for himself?

At the very least, Samantha's inheritance could

open the door to limitless possibilities for Carter as well as his unborn child.

There's nothing I wouldn't do for my son.

"Does it feel good, telling people that your son is dating a wealthy girl from Blaine? That her daddy owns a ranch and knows the governor?" Megan didn't have a lot of time.

Three days.

Or all hell could break loose if Samantha's parents followed their instincts and went after Carter and his mother. Whatever was going on with Samantha, Megan's gut was telling her that court wasn't the answer.

"I don't make a habit of gossiping about my son."

Bella hadn't answered the question.

"Okay, does it make you feel good knowing that your son is dating someone with as prominent a family as Samantha Everson has?"

"I do feel good about that," Bella said, looking her straight in the eye. "I'm thrilled that my son is a lot wiser than I am, than I ever was, and that he fell in love with a girl who has heart, compassion, drive, ambition, goals and a sense of responsibility, unlike the lowlife loser I chose."

Good answer. Rehearsed, maybe. Didn't feel like it, though. Still, she left the statement in a mental question mark column.

"Do you know why Samantha is so adamant about not going home?" Would the girl really run away rather than live at home with her parents?

Megan hadn't had that impression the day before. She'd swear that the girl had been about to agree to move back when Carter's text had come through.

Bella's headshake wasn't necessarily a negative response. "I'll let her tell you her reasons," the woman said.

"Has she said anything to you that gives you concern regarding the Eversons treatment of her?"

"I haven't asked." Another unanswered question.

"But you have to wonder, don't you?" Bella said then, looking across at Megan with concern written all over her face. "Why would a young woman choose to leave a mansion, to cook and clean when she could have a staff doing it for her, to settle for intermittent internet that's too slow for streaming, and day-old burgers instead of fresh cut steak? I know I do. Wonder, that is."

And maybe that concern was why Bella Wilson was willing to risk going to jail in order to keep the mother of her unborn grandchild safe?

Megan didn't know, but she had to find out.

As quickly as possible.

Or force Danny to file a motion that could implode everyone's lives, and leave scars that they'd carry with them forever.

Danny was ready to file the motion to get Samantha Everson home. The more people he talked to, the more convinced he became that the girl was struggling and needed help. And that her parents were the ones to get her the help she needed.

Everyone sang their praises. He'd even talked to a man that Joe had fired. The guy wasn't fond of Joe Everson, at all. He'd been ready and willing to unload about the guy as an employer, but when he heard that Danny wanted to talk about Joe as a father, the man had switched gears immediately. Had said that he was a father himself and as much of a beef as he had with the guy, he couldn't fault Joe's love for and devotion to his daughter.

That had been part of the work problem. Joe was always there for his own daughter. Would leave the farm anytime Samantha needed anything; take off from his office to attend school conferences and sport functions and doctor visits—but wouldn't always let his employees come out of the fields and barns and do the same. The former employee Danny had found had taken off anyway, to watch his child's softball game, and had been fired for doing so.

Kelly's report on Joe and Lindy was the same. She'd spent a good bit of time with each of them, separately, and in her opinion was convinced they'd each give up their lives for their daughter. Nothing mattered more to them than that she be healthy and happy.

And they both were convinced she was neither—even before she'd ended up pregnant. They feared that the pregnancy was a part of whatever scheme the Wilsons were running. That it had been an end-game, planned from the first time Carter Wilson went out with their daughter.

Kelly had called from the Eversons' ranch to let him know that she was ready to go whenever, and had relayed her opinion, including the news that she had a list of behavioral incidents, complete with dates and times, to hand over to Megan. She planned to fly back that night, and Danny was going to be leaving, too. The job in Idaho—a custody issue involving a sick child who needed a temporary change in custodial arrangements that had to be presented to the court for approval—was something he could handle quickly and be back in Wisconsin in time to file the Eversons' motion.

And if Megan succeeded in the getting the girl home, he might not have to be back at all.

The idea was a bit of a drain on his psyche and a relief, too. He was oddly not wanting to be away from Meg, and at the same time, leery of being with her.

Time apart was clearly the best option until he could recover from the sex. A couple of days should do it. It never took him more than that to move on from enjoyable physical interaction. And he'd maintained casual friendships with many of the women he'd slept with. Their call—and his.

He'd tell Meg about the side trip to Idaho as soon as he picked her up from her meeting with Samantha that afternoon, before collecting Kelly. Just in case they needed a private minute.

Privacy was key. Meg had had several hours with Samantha one on one, walking around town, having lunch, chatting. Just getting to know her.

And, hopefully establishing a sense of trust in Megan as being there strictly for her, open to whatever outcome she, in her professional opinion, thought best for Samantha. And for her unborn child, as well.

Nothing like an unexpected pregnancy to complicate already difficult situations.

The thought smacked him in the head as he pulled up to the coffee shop where he and Meg had met Samantha, before heading out to the ranch to collect Kelly.

Along with another thought or two. His memory was a little foggy in places, but he was fairly sure he'd failed to pull a condom out of his wallet the other night. Kind of remembered thinking that it wouldn't be a problem. Meg was safe after all.

With her sassy blond hair and black-and-white sexy looking suit, Meg walked out of the coffee shop with two cups in hand, balanced them as she opened the door and slid inside, handed him a cup and opened the other to put those hot lips over what he knew would be ice cold coffee. She drank black in the morning, but liked her iced concoctions in the afternoon. Different variations, but always with a sprinkle of cinnamon.

He had to tell her he was leaving.

"I have no memory of using a condom." Smooth, man.

"Thanks for sharing." She sipped. "How was your day?"

She didn't sound worried, which settled him, but…he had a responsibility to know for sure that…

"You aren't worried? I mean, I know you're on the pill and all, but…"

"This your idea of not talking, Tremaine?" They'd agreed, less than twenty-four hours before, never to mention the…episode…again.

"Just promise me that—"

"I promise," she said, cutting him off. And followed the words with, "You going to drink that coffee, or what?"

She wasn't worried.

Not about unexpected complications.

She might still be a bit afraid of losing "them" though. He'd made a promise the night before, and he intended to live by it.

He wasn't going to lose her.

He *was* going to leave her, though. Temporarily.

Before he could say so, she said, "I'm not feeling as confident that it's in Samantha's best interests to move home with her parents." Upending his business day, completely.

In all the cases they'd worked, they'd rarely seen things differently.

And not bringing Samantha home as soon as possible was one hell of a major differing.

"You're saying you need more than the few days we gave her? Because I can tell you right now, the Eversons aren't going to agree to any longer than that. And to be honest, I'm going to advise that they don't." He gave her a rundown of many of things he'd heard that day. And of Kelly's report as he drove out to the ranch. It was all information she was privy to.

And needed.

When a child was at risk, every piece of information regarding that child's past and present environments were key.

Megan listened. Something she was incredibly good at. Taking in, cataloging. Processing. One of the many talents he valued in her.

And he started to relax, as he continued to relay various conversations and key points of his day. He'd been out of whack there for a second. She'd fixed them right up.

Friendship at work.

"I did some checking, too," she said. "Everything about Bella Wilson and Carter check out. Their town is small, everyone knows everyone, and many were eager to sing Bella's praises. She works in the diner so has contact with a good half of the town on a regular basis. She grew up there, the only child of an alcoholic mother who loved her, but wasn't around, or sober much when she was. In spite of that, Bella's a great mom. Either working or with Carter, and it's been that way since she got pregnant with him her junior year of high school. She never said who the father was, and while some have speculated, it's not something anyone talks about anymore. She only made one reference about him to me, saying he was a lowlife loser. Still, by all accounts, Carter's a great kid, polite, good student, hardworking, trustworthy."

Danny's jaw tensed as he listened.

Something wasn't adding up.

Where was the magic that worked with him and Meg? In business, they'd always been able to cut through the crap and find truth together. Sometimes to the benefit of his clients, but not always, by a long shot.

This case, though…

"Are you saying you aren't going to recommend that Samantha move home? Because if that's the case, I need to let the Eversons know that we're going to be moving forward on their case sooner than planned." He could e-file the motion that night when he got to Idaho. Handle the situation there in the morning and be back in Wisconsin in time to be in court in Blaine the next morning…

Her sharp glance had him taking a deep breath. The tension running through him…probably not all about the case.

"I'm not saying that," she said. "Not at all. I'm saying...this is a lot more complicated than we thought. Samantha was respectful today. She answered my questions. I asked her if she resented how much her mother had been involved in her life, attending every track meet, etcetera, and she said she wasn't. Quite the opposite. She'd loved how much her parents had been there for her."

"But she doesn't think they're there for her now?"

"To be honest, I'm not sure what she thinks. I have the feeling *she's* not sure what she thinks. As I said, this case is a lot more complicated than we first thought."

He didn't like hearing the news. But he'd calmed enough to do his job well. And to be open to her doing hers, too. He'd been completely out of line, taking some weird kind of personal offense because they hadn't been on the same page.

They'd been on different pages many times. Their gift was leaving both versions open, discussing, seeking more information...and finally reaching the best course of action.

It wasn't about winning or losing with Meg. Or about being right.

It was about doing better together than they did alone.

About getting the healthiest result for their clients.

It wasn't Meg's fault, or Samantha's or the Eversons', or Bella's or Carter's, that expert lawyer Daniel

Tremaine was eager to do a good job and vamoose so he could cope with having made the worst mistake of his life.

He'd get over it. He had no doubt about that.

He just needed some time.

But the case needed him.

And for him, the job always came first.

Even if, in the moment, it was starting to feel like Meg did.

Chapter Eight

There days with Samantha wasn't enough. A week wasn't enough, either. Danny had been away, back to Blaine, then away again, as had Megan, flying into Wisconsin three times that next week to meet with Samantha, while spending time in Phoenix and California, too—her home base—to testify in court.

She and Danny had talked on the phone every day but hadn't seen each other since the night she'd dropped both him and Kelly at the Milwaukee airport to catch flights to different parts of the country.

The first night, back at the hotel, she'd missed him terribly. Completely out of line for anything that had gone on before. She could never remember missing anyone as much. She'd spent a good bit of the evening alternating between distraction, and analyzing herself. Plus she got some work done. But she'd utterly failed to find any help for herself.

She'd been sitting up in bed, playing a random game on her phone as an excuse to hold on to it, waiting for the call he'd said he'd make when he was in his room in Idaho.

He'd texted instead.

Because he'd hooked up?

Either way, she knew that Danny's step back was for the best. She had to get on with the rest of her life.

A life with Danny firmly in it. But not *in* it in it.

And there she was, a little over a week since she'd seen him, sitting in a cab, the shops of Milwaukee whizzing past, as she headed to the hotel where Danny would be waiting. They were due in court the following morning to determine Samantha's immediate fate.

If the judge ordered her home, the pregnant teen would be forced to leave the courthouse with her parents.

If he didn't...

He would. She *knew* he would. Had told Samantha at their last meeting two days before that he would. The Eversons had the law on their side.

But Samantha had an expert witness psychiatrist who wasn't sure moving her home right then was in the girl's best interest.

Megan.

The teenager, who'd begun to confide in her a

bit more, seemed to think that Megan's testimony would be enough to keep her with Carter and Bella.

Megan knew better. If she had sufficient, recordable reason for her opinion, maybe there'd be a chance, but she had nothing concrete.

Joe and Lindy Everson loved their daughter and wanted what was best for her. Even Samantha didn't argue with the fact.

They were great parents, willing to listen, to be patient and stay out of their daughter's counseling sessions, to trust Megan to help Samantha work through whatever was bothering her. They just needed her to live under their roof.

Their need was valid.

And one that the law said was their right.

Megan just didn't feel right about it…

And Megan was dreading what would come next.

Megan knew, though Samantha didn't, that the next step would be within hours of Samantha moving home—a motion filed for a restraining order against Bella Wilson, and one against Carter Wilson. They'd face immediate arrest and jail time if they tried to see or contact Samantha Everson.

Danny was waiting when she walked into the hotel lobby, pulling her suitcase behind her. He didn't take it from her. She didn't let go of the handle. Overwhelmed by the sudden urge to hug him, to feel his arms around her, she held on to that bag for dear life.

"Meet you in the bar in twenty?" he asked as he walked her to the elevator after check-in.

"I'll be down in five." Her plan was to quickly go down, meet up with him, then go back up again to her room within the hour.

No way she was playing with fire. Not again.

But they had to talk. To try to find the mojo that would show them some as yet unseen solution to an untenable situation for the Eversons. Once the sun rose and they headed to Blaine, the writing would be on the wall.

In her room, she made a quick stop in the bathroom, checking...as she'd been doing every time for the past couple of days...for any sign of a coming cycle.

And growing increasingly more tense when there was none. No cramps. No hint, even, of her body's usual signs of forthcoming excretion.

Headache, come on. Hit me.

What was she worried about? She'd been more than a week late more often than not in the months since she'd gone off birth control pills.

She wasn't even late yet. Just...on time.

Which she wasn't going to be if she didn't hit the elevator and speed all the way down. She might burst into tears or something equally unbecoming if she had to hand over fifty dollars to Danny Tremaine on top of everything else.

There really *were* straws that could break camels' backs, apparently.

When she made it down in time—barely—she discovered that Danny had a booth for them across the room from where they'd been seated ten days before. And as far away from the dance floor as possible.

She refused to look at the thighs that looked strong and sexy even encased in dress pants. Or the expanse of chest beneath the white shirt and striped tie.

He had an oddly small glass of wine in front of him. Obviously monitoring himself.

She ordered tea. She wasn't pregnant. Just wasn't going to tempt a fate that had turned fickle on her by drinking with Danny.

The memory of the flames they'd created hadn't dissipated enough, just yet.

"I called Kurt," she announced as she picked up a menu. It was the type of thing she might have said, oh, anytime they'd met on a job before they'd gotten naked together.

Why in the hell couldn't she get that blurry hour or two out of her brain?

She would, she reassured herself as she tried to focus on salads. Just as soon as she knew there were no consequences. That was all it was, really. Her freaking out because she'd had unprotected sex.

It wasn't like she was the first woman who'd worried about such a thing.

"You called Kurt." He was staring at her over his menu. Without any hint of a smile. "He's married. Surely you aren't thinking about trying to get back with him—"

He broke off, probably because she was looking at him like he'd lost his mind.

"I called to congratulate him on his wedding," she said. "To ask for the confirmation he'd never sent that he'd removed me from the title of his condominium..."

He sipped wine, staring more at it, at the backs of his knuckles, than at her, and she waited for him to look over.

And then said, "I asked him if he was unfaithful to me. You know, since he got married so quickly after..."

His vivid blue gaze sharpened on her, spreading warmth through her. A familiar Danny warmth. "And?"

"Once. The night we broke up. That's why he came home saying we needed to talk. He hadn't meant for it to happen, but when it did..."

"You feel better? Knowing he hadn't been screwing around on you behind your back?"

"Mostly just sad. I hate that he had to get to the point of sleeping with someone else before coming to me. Maybe we could have fixed things..."

And probably not. She knew better than that. Just wanted to hang on, to believe that she hadn't wasted three years of her life fooling herself that she had what she wanted.

Because if she could do it once, how did she know she wouldn't do it again? And again?

Like her parents had done.

Had they discovered after they married, and had her, that they weren't any more in love than she and Kurt had been?

Didn't track. They'd been inseparable until she turned ten. That birthday…they'd tried, but there'd been something missing in the celebration. It had been the first time they hadn't relived the day of her birth…talking about the beach outing, the cottage they'd rented…

"He wasn't the right guy."

"I know."

She looked at the menu again. Tried to remember which salad she'd ordered the last time they'd been there.

Had she even had a salad?

How could she remember so clearly the taste of Danny's tongue, but have no recollection of the food she'd eaten?

"You'll find him, Meg."

It took her a second to realize he was still talking about a man for her. She didn't want to talk about it.

"Samantha isn't going to thrive if she's forced back home," she blurted. "And if a restraining order is put in place… I'd bet a winning lottery ticket that she runs." She had his full attention. And liked the feeling. "As it currently stands, I don't think she's a flight risk. I honestly believe she wants help. Samantha's sure in over her head—and she maybe even knows it—but she hasn't come to the point of understanding what's going on inside her or taking control. Yet. But if you tell her she can't see Carter, the father of her baby…"

Danny took over. "But, Meg, she needs help. Obviously, she's not getting it at the Wilsons'. She's just falling deeper and deeper into parental separation there. Losing sight of reality."

Megan wanted to refute his claim.

Couldn't do so. Not because it was Danny, but because he was right.

And that got her attention, too.

Any change that might have come over Samantha, any softening, opening up, was because of Megan, not the Wilsons.

As proven by the fact that every time Samantha went back to them, and then met with Megan again, Megan had to fight the wall of defensiveness all over again. Megan had been impressed by mother and son, but there was something about their relationship with Samantha that still made her uneasy.

"He's the father of her baby and she's in love with him. Or believes she is." Megan's take was that the teenagers honestly believed themselves in love.

And who was she to say they weren't? She'd recently worked with a couple who'd been married forty years, had met at thirteen and fourteen, and were undertaking a sudden guardianship of a great-grandchild.

"Refusing to allow her access to him will be her breaking point."

"So…if we negotiate some kind of agreement whereby she moves home, assuming the court orders it, and her parents allow her to see Carter, but it has to be on their property?"

"They'd need time alone together."

"You want Joe and Lindy to allow them to have sex?"

She blinked at him. "I was thinking more of private conversation," she said. "But it stands to reason they're going to want to make out some. I'd rather leave sex out of it if we can. I think that would be best for all concerned. It's not like we're going to get that horse back in the barn. She's already pregnant. So, we don't ask for permission for them to have sex, but we don't expressly forbid it, either."

He nodded. Their waiter stopped by and they ordered. She chose a chicken salad because it sounded the least offensive. He was having pepper steak.

He loved the stuff.

A small wisp of pepper had been on his tongue…

The waitress asked if he was ready for his next flight. Megan thought they must have talked about all the traveling Danny did—since he'd checked in and out of that particular hotel a few times in the past eleven days. Maybe they'd chatted the night Danny had stayed in town when she'd been in California…

Danny nodded. The waitress, obviously taking the cue that she was interrupting, left without another word. And she said, "Samantha would need to have her phone, and be permitted to text Carter whenever she wanted to."

"That's just smart. It would give us something to trace in the event that she did run away."

Which brought up another thought. "She can't be a prisoner. If there's any chance of helping her find herself, she has to feel like she's free to come and go. She's going to have to feel like her parents trust her. And that's an almost impossible ask given the circumstances."

"I think I can help there," Danny said. "I've already been prepping them a bit, and I'd like to propose that I get an agreement written up and have it be a part of the hearing in the morning. That it's official, and Samantha hears the judge read it…"

"They'd agree to that?"

"I can't speak for them, but I'd bet my law license on it. Joe and Lindy would do anything to help their daughter. Making her feel trapped and afraid, forcing her to feel like she has to run away, is the antithesis of what they're aiming for here."

The waitress was headed their way again, with another small wineglass on his otherwise empty tray.

"Here you go," she said, setting it down in front of Danny. "It's a deeper red, made with plums, with a hint of pepper…"

Flight. He'd ordered the wine flight. She'd seen it advertised as she'd walked in the door. Four wines, four fruits, total alcohol consumption equal to two glasses of wine, twenty dollars.

The young woman reported that their food was almost ready, lifted her empty tray up to her shoulder and left them alone.

She watched Danny sip. Wondered how plum with pepper would taste. And said, "You seriously think you can get the Eversons to agree to the terms we've just laid out?"

"I do."

"I can almost guarantee you that I can get Samantha to agree to them. I'd just need to give her some kind of heads-up before court."

"I think I can arrange that, too."

Seriously.

They'd done it. Found a way to avoid implosion.

They weren't out of the woods yet. There was no telling how Carter or Bella were going to react to having Samantha out from beneath their constant control.

And there was still the major issue of getting through to Samantha, helping her express whatever it was that she was bottling up inside. Unearthing what had happened to change the confident young woman she'd been.

But they'd just given the family a chance to find their answers.

They'd done their job. Her and Danny.

As well as they always did.

Together.

"Can I have a sip of that wine?"

She wasn't pregnant. And one sip wouldn't hurt if she was.

Plum and peppers. In a glass of wine. A memory they could share.

He handed over the glass.

She took a long whiff, like a true connoisseur.

And was hit with a sudden wave of nausea so intense, she almost had to excuse herself from the table. It passed, quickly enough that she could put the glass down naturally, and say, "I think I'll pass on that one, wow!"

As soon as she felt safe, she took a sip of tea. And when the food arrived, she was able to eat without incident.

If she had the flu or had eaten something that didn't agree with her earlier in the day, the bout wouldn't have disappeared as quickly as it had come.

Or come so randomly, with such force.

Had the time to worry arrived?

Chapter Nine

The pepper steak was good. Plum wine with pepper not so much. Danny didn't finish it. And wished, like Meg, he'd never tasted it. She'd always been the more cautious, wiser one of the two of them.

He'd figured the mini flight of wine, only two small glasses, rather than the four advertised was safe, but maybe not.

When he found himself watching her lips as she forked bites between them, and getting hard under the table, he motioned for their waitress, had her take the rest of the wine, and ordered tea for himself.

They worked as they ate, laying out specific terms for the agreement he'd draw up once he got to his room. Samantha would have her curfew, but other than that she'd be free to come and go as she had in the past. She'd need to let her folks know where she was going—just in case something happened to her, they'd need to know where to start looking. Made good sense.

Carter would be welcome in the Everson home.

"Do we spell out whether or not he can stay over? Or sleep with Samantha if he does? They're sharing a room now. Are used to sleeping with each other," Meg pointed out as she attacked a chicken and greens salad that was big enough to be a meal twice over.

In spite of the obvious logic there, Danny wasn't sure he could get the Eversons to agree to their seventeen-year-old daughter sleeping with her boyfriend in their home. "What do you think?" he shot back at Meg.

"I think we leave it alone," she said. "We don't want a deal breaker on the table. We need to get Samantha home so that she has the time and space to find herself, or to help me figure out what's gone wrong inside her. How about if we put a caveat that when other issues come up, we deal with them one by one, and both parties agree to arbitration if they can't agree on something. I can be the arbitrator if they choose, but it doesn't *have* to be me."

Danny liked it. Penciled notes on his phone until he could get upstairs to his computer.

By the time they'd covered everything either of them could think of, they had a nine-item list. And he was willing to let himself be convinced that they'd firmly salvaged their friendship.

She didn't have to know that, even completely sober, he was finding everything about her unbelievably attractive. The way she used her napkin to pat her mouth, not swipe it across—who the hell noticed how people used their napkins?

"You really think that Joe and Lindy are going to agree to all of this?" Megan pulled his thoughts back to the table.

He shrugged. "They're afraid of losing their daughter. Question is, you think Samantha will be able to stick to it? She's the wild card. And with Carter influencing her..."

"I think, bottom line, Samantha wants peace. She gets defensive, belligerent, but my sense is that the outward expressions aren't bone deep. She's using them to cover up some sense of inadequacy, or fear."

And if that was the case, he was even more adamant about getting the teenager home to the parents who loved her.

"Amazing, isn't it, that even in a seemingly perfect family, with a husband and wife who not only obviously love each other, but still actually like each other, too, who enjoy being together, and adore their daughter, where money isn't even an obstacle, there are major problems. They've somehow raised a child who's no happier than you or I were..."

"I was happy when I was little," she reminded him.

"And then you weren't." He saw it every day... families hurting. Divorce, custody battles...

He couldn't risk ever being on the other side of a battle with her.

"And you still want to jump into it," he said. "You want the husband and kids." He admired her for her ability to hope for good. Wasn't sure if he'd ever had it.

But he wasn't an unhappy guy. To the contrary, he'd accepted life on his terms and enjoyed as much of it as possible.

"I do," she confirmed. "I don't know if my parents ever loved each other, or just married the wrong person, like I would have done with Kurt. Or maybe they really were in love, but one or the other of them made a mistake from which they couldn't recover."

Having sex with someone else. He knew that story.

Sex, again.

Ruining a relationship.

He had to keep his hands off Megan. Find a way to get turned off when he looked at those eyes so filled with expression, the hands that were soft and gentle, and had a good bit of strength too, he remembered as he relived them biting into his shoulders as she held on to him, riding him.

"There are no guarantees. Not in relationships or in life. But scientifically it's been proven that people need people. It's just part of who we are. Mentally, emotionally, the healthiest people are those who are surrounded by good relationships."

"I have healthy relationships." The note of defensiveness slipped in uninvited.

"Of course, you do." She seemed to take that as a given, and he sat back.

"You're the one who told me to never get married," he reminded her, just for good measure. And then wondered if she even remembered that long-ago conversation.

"I did not."

So, she didn't remember. Ironic how something that changed an entire life wasn't even on the memory radar of another.

"Sure you did," he said, cocking his head as he met her gaze. And wondered why he was pushing the issue. "I asked you what you thought a guy who enjoyed women should do to avoid breaking hearts."

"I told you that you couldn't be responsible for how other people felt, but that your best chance of not hurting anyone was to always be honest. With yourself and with whoever you were with." She coughed.

So not like her to dance around a situation. Was she struggling, too? From day one after the night they'd shared, she'd seemed so put together. So unfazed.

Other than at the thought of losing their platonic friendship.

What if she wanted him, too? Was fighting the hunger even as they sat there?

He got hard. And shut down the thought.

No.

Didn't matter who wanted who, or how badly.

Going there again would ruin them.

"I told you—"

"I remember what you told me," he interrupted, more to get his mind on the conversation and off the mental merry-go-round he kept jumping aboard. "To be honest. With myself, first. To admit what I wanted and needed. And then to be honest with women in whom I had an interest, or who showed an interest in me. To let them know what I wanted, what I was capable of giving, and not giving. To make limits clear."

She was nodding. And frowning, too. "Nowhere in there did I tell you to never get married."

Technically, no. But… "You had to know where all that honesty would lead…" No way a guy who enjoyed women, in the plural, could hook himself to one woman for life.

"You were eighteen, Danny…"

And now he wasn't. "And you think if I tell a woman that I've never been in a relationship longer than three months and that I tend to like a lot of different kinds of women, she's ever going to want to marry me? I mean, seriously, would you ever, in a million years marry a guy like that?"

The question was rhetorical. He knew the answer.

He'd been living with himself a long time.

She leaned forward, her gaze filled with compassion. He needed to look away before he got swallowed in. Lowered his gaze, caught a glimpse of soft cleavage, and jumped immediately back to the compassion. "I think, if you ever honestly wanted to marry a woman, Danny, you wouldn't want to be with different kinds of women anymore. I think when you find the right one…"

She couldn't seem to finish. He knew why.

She was a doctor.

His best friend.

And she wasn't going to lie to him.

The chances of him ever changing were slim to none.

And until ten days ago, he'd been good with that.

Megan was out of the bar as soon as she'd signed to have the tab charged to her room. Danny left her in the lobby, saying that he had to make a run to the drugstore a couple of doors down, saying he'd send her the agreement to go over when it was done. Would text her and let her know it was sent.

In days past he might have knocked on their adjoining door.

Or walked through the slightly ajar door that they'd often left unlocked between them when they were working into the night on a case.

She couldn't worry about the little changes, or nuances she might draw from them, though she did try to hold on to them as she rode the elevator up to her room as a form of distraction.

Ironic that the hour she began to honestly suspect she could possibly be pregnant with Danny's child, was the exact same hour he chose to remind her how very unsuited for each other they really were—complete with bringing up their unhappy childhoods.

If ever she'd had a sign from the heavens, that was it.

No matter what she found out, she and Danny could not marry to raise a child. Not that he would. Or she would, either. The idea was ludicrous. A disaster waiting to happen.

But even if it weren't, there was no way she would bring a child into a relationship doomed to failure. Growing up was hard enough, even with happy, well-adjusted parents.

The Eversons were a case in point.

She'd much rather raise a child in a single-parent household than do so in a home filled with unsaid words and unexpressed hurt feelings. Or, as was the case with Danny's parents, constantly expressed displeasures. Irritations. Most likely disguising hurt feelings.

Blinking back tears—borne of frustration, she wanted to believe—she put herself in time-out, squeezing into the elevator's back corner, and stared up at the floor numbers. Blinking as required by gathering moisture.

Keeping it firmly under control.

And then she was…there.

In her room's adjoining bathroom, standing at the toiletry bag hanging from the back of the door. Gazing at all of her stuff, right where she always put it.

She'd bought the test the week before, right there in Milwaukee, after taking Danny and Kelly to the airport. She'd told herself that there was nothing more she could do until day ten, so she could put the whole thing out of her mind.

Some days it had worked.

Others, she entered whatever hotel bathroom she happened to be in, caught sight of the test, and felt her insides jump up.

The night she'd spent at home in her condo on the coast of Southern California, she'd left the test packed away. And had slept well.

But then, she always slept well her first night home in her own bed.

She didn't have to take the test that night. She could leave it standing up in its pocket, right where it was. Another day or two wasn't going to hurt. And might help. Ten days post coitus was the earliest a test might come back positive. A negative response wouldn't necessarily mean there was no pregnancy.

There were cases of false positives, too.

Either way, no matter what the test said, she still wasn't going to know for sure. Not without a medical confirmation.

So, she might as well take it. If it was negative, well, good to know that so far there was no need to worry. A relief that there was still a chance that her life wasn't going to implode over one stupid mistake.

And if it was positive? Well, then, nothing to panic about. Could likely be a false result. Just a heads-up to get a medical test sometime in the near future.

A door shut close by. She heard it. Knew it was likely Danny.

Which gave her impetus to get her butt in gear. Take care of her obsession problem and be ready to work when he needed her.

She wasn't going to let him down.

So, she peed.

She waited.

And then, shaking, tearing up, sank down to the bathroom floor.

The test was negative.

Sitting at the table in his room, laptop in front of him, tie knot down to midchest and the top two buttons of his shirt undone, Danny was on item seven when he hit a snag.

They'd started their earlier conversation with Samantha only being allowed to see Carter at the Everson home. Then had determined that, in order for Samantha to trust her parents, she'd need to feel trusted, and to feel free, as though she wasn't trapped, so had determined that she have her curfew, but be permitted to come and go as she had in the past.

Problem was, she'd just gotten her driver's license a week before she'd announced her pregnancy and left home.

Bella Wilson had allowed Samantha to drive her car, but her parents hadn't given her full rein, yet. They'd only wanted Samantha to drive in their neighborhood and to and from school until she got more comfortable behind the wheel.

Which meant, if they lent her their car, she wouldn't be allowed to drive to Carter's place.

Which led to the next thing they hadn't established. Once Samantha was removed from the Wilson residence, was she to be allowed to visit?

Because if the Eversons were correct, and the Wilsons were manipulating their daughter to the point that they were going to court to get the girl out of there, it didn't make much sense for her to go back— even if just for daily visits. It would be inviting the manipulation to continue.

His fingers flew in the email he was typing to Meg. How could he convince the court that the Wilson home was not healthy for Samantha, and then say that it was all right for her to be there?

He hit send.

Grabbed his phone immediately. Texted Meg to check her email, as previously planned.

Rapped his thumb against the table as he waited.

Told himself not to picture her on the other side of the wall—maybe even in one of the various cotton pajama pants and matching T-shirts she wore to bed. Her belly doing that sexy peeking thing through the slit between the bottom of the top and the top of bottoms every time she moved.

The thought—the clear vision that hit his brain—stopped him midrap. Frozen, like a defendant on the stand who'd just been caught in a lie—he sat there.

How in the hell would he know that?

If, indeed, the first time he'd seen Meg as a sexual being, had been the night they'd had sex? It had been dark.

And she most definitely hadn't been wearing any pajamas.

Or anything else.

How could he have such a clear vision of something he'd never noticed before? And know that it was one of the sexiest things he'd ever seen?

Unless he'd been secretly lusting after his best friend, subconsciously, for years?

He sat up straight. Then stood. Paced the length of the room.

Thought like a lawyer instead of the nervous sap he seemed to be wanting to become. He was a guy. Guys noticed things.

There'd been nothing secret about it.

He just hadn't reacted to it before because he hadn't thought of Meg in a sexual way.

The turn on part had just come to the fore because...not that he was seeing her as a sexual being then...but because he had, briefly, and...he was still recovering.

The argument carried enough weight to convince him to go with it.

The sudden knock on his door—the adjoining door between his room and Meg's—had him not so sure.

Did he open it?

Was he thinking Megan wasn't safe with him anymore?

The absolute ludicrousness of that thought propelled him to the door. He could always control him. Always.

Unless he was drunk, with Megan who was drunk and unhappy, and she kissed him.

Even then. Never again.

He pulled open the door.

She was still dressed in the tight gray pants and silk, hip-length, tapered blouse she'd had on all night. Her feet were bare. And it looked like she'd washed her face.

He preferred Megan makeup free. It was how she'd always looked during their late at night tête-à-têtes.

"If we're back to normal, and I didn't ruin things,

can you explain to me why we're communicating by text and email when we're right here together? Why this door is being kept tightly closed between us? Because I have to tell you, I'm reading symbolism into that and it isn't sitting well."

He was speechless.

An occurrence so rare, he was stunned by it.

He couldn't tell her that he found even the sound of her voice alluring these days. Or that he wanted to sleep next to her completely sober.

That he was jealous of the rumpled pillow he saw on her bed behind her.

"Okay then," she started to shut her door.

"Get back here, Latimer," he said. "I have no problem with the open door. I trust myself implicitly. But I just found myself not sure about *you* and that was plain weird…"

"You don't trust me?" She actually gulped. Stood there open-mouthed.

"Of course, I do! Are you kidding me? I put as much weight in what you say as I do my own thoughts. And I'd trust you with my life above anyone else on earth. I wasn't sure that you were sure you could trust me…"

"You're feeling untrustworthy, Tremaine? Something we need to call someone about? I know a good shrink or two."

Were they having this bizarre conversation? "I know I'm trustworthy. But, yeah, I guess, when I look at me in your eyes, I'm…not sure what to see. Not sure what you see."

"I opened the door, didn't I?"

That she had.

"Then let's go to work," he told her, heading back over to the computer, needing the lifeline the job would offer him until whatever was discombobulated within him vacated his premises.

It took them five minutes to determine that they had to write in that while Samantha was free to come and go as she pleased, she was not to visit the Wilson home, the diner where Bella worked, or the town in which she and Carter lived. She'd be on the honor system, because they wanted her to feel trusted, dependable, in control and free, as much as possible, while still protecting her. And if she broke any part of the agreement, she'd be forcing her parents to take legal action to keep the Wilsons away from her.

They read the final version over together, in all its perfect legalese, and he sent it to the Eversons, who were waiting to read it and call him that night. He'd already put a call into the judge's voice mail to meet with him before court in the morning.

"Good work, Latimer," he said, as she headed toward her room.

"You, too," she told him with a smile. But instead of going through the door, she stopped, turned back to him, and he quit breathing.

"And for the record, I never, for one second, stopped trusting you…"

The rush that hit him nearly knocked him into his chair.

And wasn't sexual in nature at all.

Chapter Ten

"So I'm going to basically be on an ankle bracelet like a prisoner out of jail awaiting trial except minus the metal around my leg. That's what they call freedom and trust?"

In a black, tapered jacket pantsuit, Megan sat in the conference room at the courthouse, trying to reason with Samantha with only half an hour left before their hearing.

Trust was such a nebulous entity, elusive, intangible—and yet one of the most sought-after powers in the world. Human emotional health depended upon it.

And just last night, a nationally acclaimed lawyer had been unaware that he possessed it from the best friend he'd had for over a decade. That lack of awareness appeared to have nearly broken him there for a moment.

Megan still reeled from those seconds in Danny's room.

"This isn't your parents' stipulation, Sammie," Megan said, addressing the girl as the teenager had requested she do. *My name's Sammie, not Samantha.*

Sammie was what her parents called her. Megan found it meaningful that Sammie wasn't rejecting that, choosing a new identity, even if just another version of the name. The girl was clearly struggling to maintain her sense of identity, but could just hate the names Sam and Samantha, too.

"You can see the last bit is a write in." Megan pointed out, sitting beside the young woman at the scarred wooden table. In a midthigh-length, purple T-shirt dress, and purple flip-flops, her long wavy hair clean as it curtained her shoulders and the sides of her face, Samantha Wilson sat with her head in one hand, staring at the document Megan had placed before her.

As soon as Bella had walked into the small courthouse with the girl, Megan, who'd been waiting, had excused Samantha from the Wilsons and brought her to the room she'd secured for their use.

While the Eversons had agreed to the nine-point decree that Megan and Danny had drawn up, the judge had thrown a wrench in the works earlier that morning—requiring that Sammie carry her phone with her, and have it on with location activated, at all times that she wasn't in her parents' home, or the agreement was null and void.

Things were going to implode if she couldn't get Samantha to trust her.

Or to trust herself...

"Your mom and dad had already signed the document before it was presented to the judge," she said for the second time. "This is a court of law now, Sammie, not a battle of wills with the people you've known all your life. The judge says that there has to be measurable ways to prove malfeasance—that means you've done something wrong—in the event that you renege on the agreement, as the consequences will be steep."

She'd already explained that Samantha's parents had every right to file restraining orders against the Wilsons that day if they so chose. That everyone was trying to find other options for Samantha's sake, but that her parents were ultimately responsible for her well-being and would be held accountable if they didn't do all they could to keep her well.

The document was their attempt to do just that. If Samantha didn't follow the rules in it, her parents would go forward with a restraining order against the Wilsons. And if Sammie didn't sign the document, the motions were ready to file that day.

"I know it feels like you're between a rock and a hard place," Megan said. "I get that none of this is what you want. But you made some choices that you're going to have to stand up to, here. You want to be treated like an adult, then you need to take accountability for your part in this. Think about how your actions and choices affect others, and try to find a way to meet them partway."

"How does this meet Carter or Bella partway?"

Megan sat back, the question ringing loudly in her mind. What did the Wilsons want that this agreement wasn't giving them?

Other than Samantha in their home, the entire decree worked in their favor, out of respect for Samantha's perceived need to have her baby's father and paternal grandmother in her life.

So what else could there be?

Except the money her parents feared the Wilsons were after?

"How isn't it meeting them partway?" Megan asked, homed in completely.

"They're being treated like pariahs."

Megan listened for more. Some explanation that could give her real insight. Was disappointed when it didn't come.

"In the eyes of the law, Bella Wilson is harboring a fugitive. A runaway. Your parents aren't pressing charges, and they're willing to keep everything else out of court as well. More than that, Carter is free to come and go in their home. Your home. This decree makes it possible for you and Carter to be together, to remain in constant communication. You'll be allowed to see Bella. To come and go as you have done before the trouble started."

"I can't go home. And if I have lunch at the diner like we've been doing, they get arrested."

Home. She was calling the Wilsons' place home. She'd been staying there less than a month.

"They'd be served with orders to appear in court," she corrected. "They wouldn't go to jail unless they failed to follow any orders that followed. You don't have to sign the form, Sammie. You can take your chance that my testimony will sway the judge enough to allow you to remain with the Wilsons. Or you get sent home with your parents with no agreement in effect. I can understand that it's hard for you to see the good in this, but the decree is only here for you. To give you assurances that your needs are being considered. You and I will still be talking. I'm not abandoning you, and neither are your parents. I can't speak for Bella or Carter, but I'd guess that they have no intention of doing so."

It was all for her. That's what Megan needed the young woman to see.

Or, more importantly, to feel.

"Hopefully, as we work together, we can figure out how to communicate what's bothering you so much at home and see if we can make things better."

The pressure of being pregnant going into her senior year of high school was enough in and of itself.

Megan was almost twice Samantha's age, independent, and financially comfortable and she'd been panicked about being pregnant.

For a seventeen-year-old girl…

Samantha wasn't showing yet, but as Megan watched the girl deliberate, sat with the silence that had fallen, a twinge of envy shot through her. Freezing, she forced her mind to go blank while all emotion dissipated. Was she actually jealous of a critically troubled child?

Because Samantha was carrying a child and she was not?

She shook her head. Yeah, the tears the night before had come as a bit of a shock. But they hadn't been about her not carrying Danny's baby, had they? They'd been tears of relief.

Which made her wonder, did Samantha really want the baby she carried? She claimed she did. Adamantly. But if she was being manipulated…maybe it was more than just love they were holding over her. Were Carter and Bella guilting her into being a mother when the girl might more likely opt to give the child up for adoption?

It was definitely an angle they needed to cover.

At another point.

The girl sat silently. Staring. A knock on the door—Danny, she knew by arrangement—let Megan know they had ten minutes until they had to be in court. And she relayed as much to Sammie.

HARLEQUIN®
Reader Service

FREE BOOKS GIVEAWAY

See Details Inside

Dear Reader,

I am writing to announce the launch of a huge **FREE BO GIVEAWAY**... and to let you know that YOU are entitled choose up to FOUR fantastic books that WE pay for.

Try **Harlequin® Special Edition** books featuring comfor and strength in the support of loved ones and enjoying journey no matter what life throws your way.

Try **Harlequin® Heartwarming™ Larger-Print** books featuring uplifting stories where the bonds of friendshi family and community unite.

Or TRY BOTH!

In return, we ask just one favor: Would you please participate in our brief Reader Survey? We'd love to he from you.

This FREE BOOKS GIVEAWAY means that your introducto shipment is completely free, <u>even the shipping</u>! If you decide to continue, you can look forward to curated mor shipments of brand-new books from your selected serie always at a discount off the cover price! <u>Plus you can ca any time</u>. Who could pass up a deal like that?

Sincerely

Pam Powers

Pam Powers
For Harlequin Reader Ser

Complete the survey below and return it today to receive up to 4 FREE BOOKS and FREE GIFTS guaranteed!

FREE BOOKS GIVEAWAY
Reader Survey

1

Do you prefer stories with happy endings?

○ YES   ○ NO

2

Do you share your favorite books with friends?

○ YES   ○ NO

3

Do you often choose to read instead of watching TV?

○ YES   ○ NO

YES! Please send me my Free Rewards, consisting of **2 Free Books from each series I select** and **Free Mystery Gifts**. I understand that I am under no obligation to buy anything, no purchase necessary see terms and conditions for details.

❏ **Harlequin® Special Edition** (235/335 HDL GRM5)
❏ **Harlequin® Heartwarming™ Larger-Print** (161/361 HDL GRM5)
❏ **Try Both** (235/335 & 161/361 HDL GRNH)

FIRST NAME | LAST NAME

ADDRESS

APT.# | CITY

STATE/PROV. | ZIP/POSTAL CODE

EMAIL ❏ Please check this box if you would like to receive newsletters and promotional emails from Harlequin Enterprises ULC and its affiliates. You can unsubscribe anytime.

SE/HW-122-FBG22_SE/HW-122-FBGVR

BUSINESS REPLY MAIL
FIRST-CLASS MAIL   PERMIT NO. 717   BUFFALO, NY

POSTAGE WILL BE PAID BY ADDRESSEE

HARLEQUIN READER SERVICE
PO BOX 1341
BUFFALO NY 14240-8571

NO POSTAGE
NECESSARY
IF MAILED
IN THE
UNITED STATES

"It's only until I'm eighteen. Then Carter and I can get married."

Megan waited. The choice had to be Samantha's.

"What if I forget to charge my phone?"

"Outside of school hours, or unless you're with your parents, you stay home." The point was clear. "You're going to have to take responsibility on that one. But seriously, you're planning to be a mother in a little more than six months. And if you can't handle the small responsibility of remembering to keep your phone charged, or stay home if it's not, how on earth are you going to be able to take on the responsibilities of caring for a child?"

Samantha picked up the pen and signed her name.

They were in and out of the courtroom in less than five minutes. A private meeting with the judge and his personnel, with only the three Eversons and Danny and Megan present. A new copy of the decree was presented, signed by all parties and notarized, and Samantha agreed to leave with her parents. No hearing necessary.

The teenager hadn't had a chance to communicate with Carter and Bella Wilson before the meeting, purposely. But as the party of five exited, Danny in front with the Eversons and Megan and Samantha in the rear, the other two were waiting outside the courtroom, presumably to be allowed to enter for the hearing.

Danny tensed, ready to inform the Wilsons that Samantha would be leaving with her parents, letting them know that they'd face action if they tried to intervene, but Megan pushed in front of him.

"Sammie, would you like a chance to talk to Carter and his mom?" she asked, looking only at her client. Leaving Danny, he knew, to deal with his.

Samantha had exchanged a worried glance with her parents when she'd first entered the courtroom, and they'd yet to speak to each other. But they'd given their daughter the right to communicate with Carter at her pleasure.

Danny knew Megan was worried about the young couple running, and was trying to do everything she could to circumvent that eventuality. He hoped her faith in Samantha panned out. For the Eversons, but also for her.

She took her cases to heart. Would go hard on herself if she failed her young charge. It was something he'd always known, but he'd never felt such a strong streak of protectiveness as he watched her take charge of the volatile situation.

As it turned out, she hadn't needed his machismo. While Samantha had a couple of minutes alone with Carter and Bella, Megan had a quiet conversation with Lindy and Joe, assuring them that the decision to sign the agreement had been Samantha's, and giving them a short overview of the teen's comments and concerns. She encouraged them to be open to

listening to whatever Samantha might have to say
to them, to give her their truth, but not to argue with
hers. Gave them her card and told them that she
would stay in town for the next several days, with
daily sessions scheduled with Samantha to make sure
that the transition home went smoothly.

Might not be typical protocol, but she wasn't a
typical therapist. They'd hired her private expertise
for what exclusive care Samantha needed in the moment, along with future sessions as well.

And then, while Samantha and Carter had a moment alone together, with Carter looking extremely
concerned, Bella, in a short blue skirt and white T-
shirt top, approached the rest of the adults, handing
a piece of paper to the Eversons. "If my son is ever
a problem, or if there's a problem with the baby, I'd
appreciate you giving me a call," she said, and then,
without waiting for a response, turned and walked
down the hall.

She'd obviously told her son she'd wait for him
outside. Or just assumed he'd know that she would.
For all Danny knew they'd driven separately.

He and Megan had not. Which meant that half an
hour later, they were in their rental, heading back
to Milwaukee for him to catch a flight out of town.
He was heading home to his condo in Colorado for
the night, then handling a case there starting the
next day.

Unless the decree that had just been signed was broken, Danny was done in Blaine.

And had no idea when he'd be seeing Meg again.

A circumstance completely normal to them.

And yet one that was leaving him decidedly unsettled. He wanted to believe the reason for his unusual discomfort was because they'd had such a close call with their relationship the week before. Knew that was at least part of it.

Hoped that was *all* of it.

Danny stopped for coffee on the way out of town. She was on the phone when he got back to the car. He reached to hand her the cup of iced coffee she'd requested, pulling his hand back a bit too swiftly when their fingers brushed, and elbowed the bag she'd had sitting on the console during her call, causing it to fall to the floor behind them.

Setting his cup in the holder, he immediately got back out and dove into the back seat to retrieve her belongings—feeling like an inexperienced schoolboy and hoping she didn't notice.

Meg's satchel, which doubled as her purse, had been a Christmas present from him several years before. One he'd actually replaced, on another gift occasion, but which she'd asked him to return because she loved the original one. It had just the right pockets for everything, she'd said that long ago gift exchange day. One he couldn't remember in detail.

But he remembered her showing him every pocket and what went in it.

He remembered one pocket in particular, for no good explainable reason.

The pocket for her birth control pills.

It was empty. Meaning the little snap-over case she kept to carry them had to have fallen under the seat. He searched. Under both sides. Front and back.

And heard her end her call.

"What's going on?" she asked, peering over the seat before taking a sip of her coffee. She had her bag in her lap, returning things to their rightful places.

"I can't find your birth control case. Of all things to…" He dove in again, his suited rib cage gouged by the cup holder on the floor in the back of the front console. "It has to be here…it's not like…"

"I'm not on the pill anymore."

He froze in place, cup holder pain and all, and then slowly climbed back out of the car, his heart rate thundering in his ears.

He wasn't angry.

Wasn't…anything.

Except speechless. Shocked.

Blank-minded.

Sliding back into the front seat, seeing his coffee cup there, his mind started to work again. "Come again?"

"It's okay, Danny. I didn't say anything before

because…well…why? Unless there was something to worry about. And there isn't."

"There isn't." He stared at her, at the openness of her gaze as she held his.

"No," she said, and then, as she flashed a smile, looked away. "I took a test just to be sure, and it came back negative."

She'd worried, and handled it on her own, he translated. He was slightly pissed. Knew he had no right to be. Or good reason to be.

"What happened that night was on both of us. Equally. You should have come to me, let me know you were concerned…"

"I wasn't," she said, and then admitted, "not much anyway. I just took the test so I wouldn't worry."

That sounded like her.

"And it was negative."

"Yep."

Good. That was good. A blessing for which he could be thankful.

As soon as he had enough brain muscle working to wrap his mind around the whole thing.

"You still could have told me," he said then, starting the car and heading them out of town before he did too much thinking in wrong areas.

Like imagining if she *had* been pregnant with his child.

God, what a mess that would have been. Him, putting Meg in that position. Wouldn't anyone who'd known them in college get a laugh about that? The irony of it.

A couple of silent miles down the road, he asked, "Isn't it a little soon?"

"For what?"

"A test."

"They can tell at ten days now."

Modern science and all. Still, sounded early.

"Have you had your period?" Not a usual them question, at all, but he didn't much care at the moment. She'd been worried that they'd created a baby together and hadn't told him.

He'd even opened the door to the conversation when he'd told her he hadn't worn a condom. In case, in her alcohol-induced state she had noticed. Or remembered.

Just because he remembered every second of their bodies together—more coming back to him in odd moments over time—didn't mean she remembered any of it at all...

It took him a second to realize she hadn't answered his question.

"Meg?"

"No," she said, then turned to him. He could only glance her way, but he felt her earnest expression trained on him. "But, seriously, Danny, the test is known to be basically accurate, with margin for error, of course, but it was more than ten days, and if I didn't have raised levels of the hCG hormone by then, I'm fine."

"You haven't had a period. That's not fine."

"My cycle's been messed up since I went off the pill."

Finally. Something logical to hang on to. To turn his face away from the fear for a second.

"You'll let me know if that changes?"

"My cycle?"

He didn't respond. And she quietly answered him. "Yes."

He glanced her away again. Wanted to reach over and take her hand.

A mostly idiotic response to one more sign that they'd managed to escape permanent damage from their night of going off the rails.

He reached for his coffee instead.

Chapter Eleven

"I have a confession."

Three days had passed since she'd seen Danny, and Megan smiled when she answered his call to the greeting. Sitting up on her hotel room bed, pillows propped behind her while she read from an online journal full of teenage pregnancy psychological studies, she said, "What'd you do now?"

He'd called each of the three nights he'd been gone, conceivably checking up on Samantha's sessions, because he genuinely cared, but also in case he needed to make time in his schedule to get back to Blaine to file the restraining order against the Wilsons.

So far, there'd been no indication that such a move would be necessary.

"I'm being serious."

She straightened. "What'd you do?" she asked, getting worried. If he'd gotten himself into some kind of trouble...

Danny was about as straight an arrow as they made.

Unless... "Does this have to do with a woman? Did you sleep with someone I know?" She'd been peeved a time or two when he'd had liaisons with mutual acquaintances, fearing the woman would be hurt.

God, let it not be someone from Sierra's Web.

God, let her not be hurt that he'd slept with someone else.

Or worse, envious.

He had to do it. She wanted him to do it. Part of the recovery plan. Get them back on normal footing. Him with other woman, her not wanting to be one of them.

"I liked it."

Okay, fine. That was a given. But... "Who is she?"

"I liked it with you, Meg. And I feel like an ass. You're my best friend and I feel like some kind of slime for... I get these random...thoughts...memories...and I shouldn't be thinking of you that way. I swear to God I never have before. And I'm sure it's going to fade...just... I had to tell you because otherwise I'm just a creep over here entertaining inappropriate thoughts in my mind."

Her body flooded with warmth. Megan struggled to hold the phone—and get her mind into professional mode. To deal with a person in mental distress. To help him.

"It was good." The words weren't professional. Or anything she'd have normally chosen to say. "It's kind of a given that you'd have liked it, Danny. It was you. Have you ever had sex where it wasn't good?"

"I don't know. Probably not."

"Because you enjoy it and you pay attention that your partner does, too." She'd heard that about him. More times than she'd wanted to. But she also now knew, firsthand, how very true the assertion was. Danny hadn't just taken his own pleasure, he'd watched her face, moving in various ways, and when he'd hit an exact mark, he'd seemed to know. And to be able to extract more and more pleasure from it. Doing different things there. In ways she'd never heard of.

Her panties were getting wet just thinking about it. And that information was definitely only to be part of the conversation inside her head. There was no good to come out of sharing.

She'd get over it.

"So, you remember it?"

If only she could be so blessed as to not.

"Of course, I do."

"And it…was good for you?" His voice, so soft… vulnerable even…she squeezed her toes, crossed her legs, held on tight.

"It's you, Tremaine, what did you expect?"

"On a scale of one to…" His tone had changed, lightened.

"Shut up."

"Compared to others…"

"Daniel, Tremaine if you don't stop, I'm hanging up on you."

He got serious then and asked about Samantha. They discussed Megan's impressions of the girl's continued defensiveness against her parents, her inability to settle back into their home with any kind of ownership or sense that she belonged there. But there were no immediate issues. Carter had been over every day. He was polite and respectful to Samantha's parents. She hadn't challenged any directive they'd given her.

"But you're concerned."

"Very."

"How long you planning to stay?"

She wasn't sure. She had even turned down another job because of that. "Another few days, at least."

"Everything else okay?"

Was she pregnant? She read into the words.

"Everything's fine."

She hadn't had her period yet. She'd been six

weeks late on her previous cycle. "You need to let it all go, Danny," she said, taking pity on him. "Move past it."

Lord knew she was trying desperately to do so.

And the current conversation was making it extremely difficult not to dwell.

They talked more about his current case. About the great steak he'd had for dinner.

"I miss you," he said then. And she stiffened again.

"You been drinking?" That would explain the bizarre start to the conversation, too. The confession.

"Other than the ill-fated wine flight the other night, and an occasional beer, I haven't touched a sip of alcohol since our first night in Blaine."

There it was again.

That night that wouldn't let them go.

But they had to let go of it. So, she regaled him with a boring story about her mother's husband trying to fix a faucet, flooding the bathroom, and needing to call a plumber. Asked if he'd talked to his parents.

Heard about some ongoing argument they were trying to get him to weigh in on as to whether or not they should take a cruise or a tour of Greece for their next vacation—both of them pulling out all the stops to get him on their side. It would be funny if they weren't perfectly serious in their struggle to get their own way. If they didn't fight ugly.

"I offered to finance one of the trips so Mom

could tour Greece and Dad could go on his cruise," he told her. "And Dad went off on Mom for putting me in that position, absolutely refusing to take my money and telling her if she did, he wouldn't be there when she got back from her trip."

Oh, Lordy.

He mentioned a mutual friend, then, having run into him, found out he was divorced. They'd both seen it coming. The guy had been married four times, and the last wife had been ten years older than him and wanting to live off the land in the middle of nowhere. Since he was a city guy through and through that writing had been on the wall.

He had a business call come in then. One he had to take.

And as she was about to say goodbye, she said, "Danny?"

"Yeah?"

"I'd give it a ten."

He'd needed a pick-me-up.

And she'd needed to be as honest with him as he'd been with her. She'd never doubted that sex with Danny would be great.

What she'd known was that sex between them would ruin the very special friendship they shared, and she'd rather die than live without it.

Danny had just hung up the phone two afternoons later when he saw a call from Meg coming through.

In his home office in Denver, he glanced out the high-rise window looking out toward Pike's Peak, and answered the call.

"We have a problem."

"I know. I just got off the phone with the Eversons." Free hand in his pocket, he moved to the wall of windows, taking in the city more than the mountains in the distance. He was hoping he and Meg had worked their usual miracle and Samantha would reconnect with her real life and settle back in at home.

"Samantha called me. She's got a fair point, Danny," Meg told him, as he'd expected she would.

"According to Joe and Lindy, there's been no softening in her toward them. No indication that she's doing anything but existing in their space until she's free to go. It's like she's been brainwashed and they can't reach her."

"She's been home less than a week. Mental conditioning, if any exists, is going to take more than five days to unravel," she reminded him. He'd expected that, too. But they had to talk it through. It was what they did. And how they found solutions.

But right now, he couldn't. He just needed some time apart from mental connection with her. His best friend was suddenly like a bad cold—Danny couldn't seem to shake her effect on him.

Her voice, her body, thoughts of her, the feel of her, kept popping up in odd moments throughout his days—and his nights. It was like some foe he couldn't shake and didn't know how to fight. He'd never encountered this before—never been up against a problem he couldn't either fix or distance himself from.

Except maybe his parents.

And he had put a lot of distance between them.

When Danny had discovered that Megan wasn't on the pill after he'd known she wasn't pregnant, the idea that they'd taken that risk, that Megan Latimer could have been carrying his baby...

Like a drug that he'd erroneously taken that was having a permanent effect on his system, he couldn't devoid himself of the concept. It was consuming him.

Nor was he getting the time and space he needed to recover his equilibrium. And now, the Everson case had thrown another wrench in the works.

"Lindy not only had every right, but also a duty, to get her daughter the medical attention she needs."

"Samantha had already seen a doctor at the free clinic in Milwaukee. She has prenatal vitamins and didn't need to be seen again for another few weeks," Meg replied.

"She needed to be seen by the obstetrician who will be caring for her and delivering her baby. Samantha's young, and Dr. Cambrie advised that it was important that she see Samantha right away so that she can monitor her from the beginning, to have measurements..."

"The doppler recording of the heartbeat, the rest

of the doppler exam and measurements, could have been scheduled for a time later in the week, as Samantha had requested as soon as she caught wind of what was going on."

"They were in the doctor's office, Meg. It was part of the routine three-month exam, and while it was scheduled as an initial exam, Samantha's three months pregnant, so it made sense to do it all."

"Maybe it was logical if you look at it that way, but Samantha had told Carter he could be there the first time she heard the heartbeat. She wanted him there. He had a right to be there. He's the baby's father. Think about that for a second. Fathers have rights. And hearing your baby's heartbeat for the first time, that's a big thing. And while we might not like Bella's inclusion, at this point, in Samantha's mind, Bella's a soon to be grandmother to her child, just like her own mother is. Her mother was there, so Bella should have had the right as well."

"She got her way." The exam was rescheduled. Because after Samantha's request to wait had been denied, she'd gotten hard and implacable, absolutely refusing to cooperate with anyone for anything. She wouldn't submit to any of the lab work that was to have been done.

He couldn't think about baby heartbeats and how, as a father, it felt to hear it for the first time. He had to look at the law. That was his job.

What he was good at.

"And we likely lost whatever leverage we'd gained with her in terms of trust." Meg's tone wasn't encouraging. She sounded…angry. "I'm on my way to see her now," she said, which meant she was talking to him over the car's hands-free calling system.

And he had to tell her… "Joe and Lindy are seriously considering giving up on reaching Samantha at the moment. They fear that she's too far gone and that the only way to get their daughter back is to prevent Carter and Bella from having any contact with her. The continuous contact with Carter is allowing him to keep his hooks in her."

"I'll have to testify that I don't think that's in Samantha's best interests."

"I know, and so do they. They very much want you to keep working with their daughter. They feel that you're good for her, and their theory is that when Samantha hears you testify on her behalf, that makes you a good guy in her world, which will make her more apt to confide in you when she's ready." The distraught parents had thought it all through.

"Her allowed contact with Carter is giving her the strength to open her mind to other perspectives, to considering that her parents aren't all bad or wrong." Meg's reply was firm. Unbending, even. "We've made some progress, Danny, but you don't rebuild trust in a few days. She's been more open to seeing their side, to seeing signs that they're loving, wonderful people who want what's best for her, but she doesn't trust it yet. Trust takes time to build, you know that. And what Lindy did today, surprise attacking her with hearing the heartbeat for the first time, without giving her time to even let Carter know...that just blew whatever trust we'd been building. They're going to shove her straight into Bella's and Carter's seemingly loving arms. Even if their intentions were good."

"Not if there's a restraining order out against them. After this past week, living with a daughter who seems like a stranger in their home, and then the scene at the doctor's office today, they're convinced that the only way to get Samantha back is to cut her off from Carter completely."

"She'll run away."

"They're prepared to hire a bodyguard." While the idea had sounded a bit drastic to him at first, he wasn't sure it was overkill. He thought about some of the cases he knew where kids had been groomed, essentially brainwashed, into horrible situations that they thought they wanted and needed...

And, in his own current bewildered personal state, he found himself wondering how he'd feel if he was in their position—a parent whose child had suffered a sudden and drastic change of personality and who was being clearly influenced by an outside source— he'd do the same.

As quickly as possible.

"Unless you can somehow convince me differently, I have to advise them to file the motion for the restraining order. They want it in place before Samantha's next appointment."

"I'm in Blaine now. Can you give me a day or two, at least? Let me see what I find when I get inside." She'd been meeting with Samantha in a private conference room at the local library because it was impartial space, basically soundproof, and without a viewing window.

But wasn't a medical facility that would make the girl feel more like something was wrong with her, which could put her defenses up. Samantha seemed to believe that there was nothing wrong with her, but that everyone who didn't agree with her was wrong.

Typical behavior for someone being brainwashed or manipulated.

He'd seen Meg work miracles before...

"I know I can get you today, at the very least." It wasn't much.

He had no better answer.

And Samantha was waiting for her.

After hanging up, Danny went to a treadmill he hadn't used in months, turned the speed up a notch from his norm, hopped on and tackled the challenge with impressive success.

He was not a man who liked to fail.

And was starting to feel failure coming at him from all sides.

Chapter Twelve

Megan did not do well when life felt as though it was flying out of control. She knew the importance of emotional and mental equilibrium to good health and happiness and had long ago determined that she would always do all she could to keep herself on the path to joy.

Life was too short to waste.

She'd started out her time in the world blissfully happy—to the point that she'd dedicated her life to helping struggling children find even a semblance of the kind of happiness she remembered—or at the very least, helping them have peaceful hearts.

And so…after a tense hour with Samantha, she took herself shopping, looked at pretty things, color-ful displays, delicious looking fancy goods in bak-

ery cases. She cleared her mind for a while, paying
attention to a nice scent when she passed a perfume
counter, to music as she rode an escalator. To the
taste of the cinnamon in the iced drink she ordered.

Then, on the way back to her hotel, she made a
stop at the drugstore a few doors down. She still
hadn't had her period, and it was time to make certain she was just dealing with an off cycle. The first
test, at ten days, could have been false. Probably
hadn't been, but she had to rid herself of the possibility—clear her heart of the niggling idea of what-
if—and reclaim her joy.

Maybe it was time to reevaluate, to seek out new
joy. To take up sailing. Or start dating again. Or…
eat a cookie.

On her way out of the drugstore, she picked up
a small pack of her childhood favorite chocolate
sandwich cookie and dropped her purchases in her
satchel.

She had to call Danny.

Had to figure out how to save Samantha and her
parents from an impending fatal collision.

And to give them all her best, she had to clear
her mind first.

Cookies on the bathroom counter, ready for her
immediate consumption, a rush of momentary pleasure, she peed on the stick.

Washed her hands.

Grabbed the cookies and stepped out into the hotel

room as she opened the pack and bit into the first, round piece of crunchy delight. She wasn't going to hover.

Or obsess.

She was on the road to sliding back inside her best self.

Checked her watch. Chewed. Looked out the window to the bustling street below. Heard a door shut close by. Thought of Danny having been next door earlier in the week.

Wondered if he'd be back soon.

Missed him.

Chewed. Had a little trouble swallowing past the dryness in her throat and grabbed a bottle of water out of the mini fridge. Downed it.

Bit off another piece of cookie—into her second one—and wandered back toward the bathroom.

The skinny plastic apparatus was there. On the counter. Right where she'd left it.

She wasn't going to cry this time.

She was moving on. Past the craziness of past weeks. Into the life she wanted.

She could have a baby any time she chose. There were sperm banks aplenty in California.

And she was probably going to start dating again.

With a cookie in one hand, she dipped inside the bathroom door and got a peek at the stick. It would only take a second.

She could throw the thing out later.

When she was done eating.

And...

Two lines?

There were two lines?

The cookie dropped to the floor. She was peripherally aware that she managed to step on it, as she got a closer look—then picked up the stick for certain confirmation.

Two lines?

Carrying the thing out to the bedroom and over to the window, she held it up to the light, looking for the mistake.

Read the box again. Test line there, one or two lines there. Even had a diagram.

Two lines.

Clearly, two lines.

She was pregnant?

Free hand on her stomach, she looked at the stick again. Stood in front of the mirror, saw herself standing there, hand on her completely flat stomach, stick in her other hand.

Yeah, it was really her.

She held the stick up.

Saw two lines in the mirror.

And when her knees started to feel a little weak, dropped down to the end of the bed.

She was pregnant.

Danny's baby was growing inside her.

And, God help her, she was little bit happy about that.

Shaking, she continued to hold the stick.

Thought about telling him.

And her joy fled.

She was going to lose him.

Unless…

Could they, maybe, be best friends who didn't get married, or have sex, but raised a happy healthy child together?

She was going to lose him. He was a wonderful person—her best friend—but her baby's father?

She couldn't wrap her mind around how that would look. Or could possibly work.

And she couldn't fathom a life without Danny in it.

Watched as a tear fell to the stick in her hand, splashing off the plastic casing. And then another. She had to throw it away but didn't get up. Didn't want to let go of it.

Or of the first thrill of joy she'd felt before reality had come crashing in.

No way Danny was going to be okay with the news. He'd feel guilty as hell. Would need to tend to the baby, to the child, would feel trapped, would probably try to be something he was not.

And how did you enjoy the unfettered company of various women with a child in your life?

He knew who and what he was. Knew how to live his true life without hurting others. That was why he was single.

Oh, God. There was no way out.

She needed her best friend, but he was the other side now.

She didn't trust him to be there for her.

And couldn't be there for him, either, because she was the other side now, too.

She'd had sex with Danny.

She was pregnant.

She had effectively ruined his life.

And the best friendship she'd ever had.

Danny's two days at home were cut short with a phone call. He was already at the airport in Denver, getting ready to check in for his flight to Milwaukee, when Meg's ID came up on his cell. He'd been rushed, booking the last-minute flight, and had planned to call her when he got to the gate.

She'd worked her magic again, in that she'd been able to help Samantha see that she was only hurting herself, and her cause, by making herself so disagreeable with her parents. She'd had a talk with them after her session with Meg that day, had been seemingly more open to their side of the conflict, to trying to see their point of view as well as her own, then had asked for an amendment to their decree.

She wanted Carter to have father rights written into the decree. Just as he'd be financially responsible for child support when the baby was born, he also had the right to be a part of bringing his child into the world. She wanted it in writing that her parents weren't allowed to deny him the privileges that an expectant father could reasonably expect to enjoy.

His conversation with Meg was brief, confirmation that he was on his way, he'd be getting in late that night and would see her for breakfast in the morning.

And yet, even with the brevity, he felt like something was off. A tone in her voice. Or maybe lack of one. None of their usual warmth.

She'd claimed a victory that day, had snatched a child back from what she'd seen as the jaws of death to any imminent chance of happiness, but she hadn't seemed pleased.

And he was getting so far from the self he knew he was starting to not recognize himself. Meg was tired. He'd been in line at security. They'd said what they had to say in a hurry, before he had to give his phone over to the little plastic bowl that would take it through surveillance.

Shaking off the impression, he got on with his business. He'd managed to get the room next to hers that he'd occupied days before, and after he entered quietly so as not to disturb her, he smiled at the adjoining door, glad to know she was close. Then he crashed before he did something counterproductive like picture her splayed out across her sheets with that little slit of belly showing between her pajama pants and top.

The next morning, sitting across from Meg at breakfast in the restaurant off the lobby where they'd first met Lindy and Joe Everson, he watched her smile as she ordered her oatmeal and toast, and only had brief thoughts about the minimal amount of cleavage showing where the V-neck of her blue-and-white jacket buttoned at the top. He'd been with her ten whole minutes without his body betraying him.

And things between them were perfectly fine. She'd teased him about the fact that his hair was still wet when he approached, and he'd told her that wet was better than standing up on end. Their eyes had met. They'd smiled.

Back to normal.

He'd been right to ignore his uncharacteristic concerns in the airport the night before after their brief phone call.

Or so he thought. Until he noticed that while she'd gone through two glasses of orange juice, she wasn't drinking coffee.

And wasn't meeting his gaze across the table much, either.

When, after he'd had her taste his lobster frittata because she was a lobster aficionado, she barely got a chew in before she got up and made a beeline for the bathroom, he knew.

Clear as day, it hit him.

Maybe he'd taken on a new clairvoyancy along with fatherhood.

Or had known since he'd enjoyed Meg's body so much that night that fate would be making him pay for it.

And something else socked him in the face, too. She knew.

No coffee. No morning caffeine?

For Meg?

She knew. And she hadn't told him.

She didn't think him worthy of the news? Hadn't trusted him enough to handle it?

Didn't want him to know?

Didn't want him to be the father of her child?

Wasn't planning to have it?

He shook his head on that one. Meg was just one of those women who would have the baby. It was who she was.

Sometimes being a girl's best friend meant you knew her too well, apparently.

Sometimes being her best friend sucked.

Most particularly when it meant you were going to lose her.

The thought brought a sense of weakness he couldn't afford, and he made a quick, mental switch back to the fact that she'd known and hadn't told him.

A wave of anger surfaced. Passed all the way through him. He let it linger. Held on to it.

Anger was better than...

Hurt?

Because it did hurt.

The fact that she hadn't told him.

And the fact that...

There she was. Coming toward him as though everything was normal.

Four tables away. Damn her for letting him order his breakfast thinking that.

Three tables away. Damn him for not using a condom.

Two tables away. Damn him way more for drinking so much he didn't stop himself from having sex with her.

But first, she was going to answer to keeping her condition a secret from him. How dare she sit there and argue Carter Wilson's rights as a father and...

She looked him straight in the eye as she took her seat. And the expression there...the compassion, the sorrow, stopped the angry words about to escape his lips.

"I'm pregnant, Danny. I didn't mean to have this conversation here. I just found out last night. Wanted to wait to tell you in person, but not like this. Then the lobster...and... I'm so sorry."

Her apology dashed his anger, leaving him with a cacophony of thoughts and emotions swirling into a confusing fog.

"You're sorry that you're pregnant? Or that it's my baby?" That apology. It was there. He had a hold of it.

"I'm sorry that you're in the position of father-to-be when I know it's the absolute last thing you want for your life. When you've expressly chosen not to be a man with a family because you know it's the best and happiest route for you to take for yourself and for others."

He didn't need her psychiatry talk. He needed his friend.

But when he met her gaze, he slid into blankness. Not home.

"And I'm sorry for our friendship," she continued, seeming to try to get him to understand something he wasn't yet seeing.

Everything inside him told him he didn't want to see what she was going after.

Was that how her patients felt when she was trying to pull things out of them? Was she ever wrong in what she thought was there?

He sure as hell hoped she was. Even if it was just this one time.

"I didn't think there was anything that would ever rock us," she said then, sounding as lost as he felt. He needed to get out of there, to go call his best friend.

Except there she was, sitting across from him, and he couldn't reach her.

"We need to talk about this, obviously, but right now we have to go," she said, shaking her head. "We can't be late."

She hadn't eaten much. Neither had he, but he wasn't eating for two. Nor had he just lost the contents of his stomach, which he presumed she'd just done.

Had it happened before?

Was she going to have a rough time of it?

Questions started to appear in the swirl of confusion, but that wasn't the time to ask them.

"Just one thing," he said as he motioned for their bill. "I never said that I didn't want to be a father. Only that I didn't want to marry."

The distinction hadn't been something she'd picked up on in the past. Probably because, to her, the two were pretty much synonymous.

Until that morning, that difference of perception hadn't mattered.

And then it did.

Chapter Thirteen

Because Samantha dropped her defensiveness and showed her parents her true feelings regarding Carter's paternal rights being honored, Joe and Lindy immediately capitulated and added a tenth item to the decree. Their openness to seeing their daughter's needs, to trying to understand her, and to meeting her needs made the future look brighter.

And gave Megan a much-needed reminder.

Things weren't always going to fit in pretty little boxes. Life, with all of its people with their own individual emotions and needs and wants, was messy.

And still beautiful.

Megan met with Samantha at the library while Danny took care of getting the amended and notarized decree filed, then they were heading back to Milwaukee. She would remain in town at least a few more days, and then make trips back and forth at least twice a week. Danny had suggested the possibility of virtual meetings, at one point when Samantha had excused herself to the restroom, but the Eversons had quickly negated that plan. With Megan's full support.

Her presence clearly gave Samantha security, was something the young woman trusted, and until they got to the root of whatever was driving her, Megan's physical presence mattered. She was further pleased by the fact that the Eversons answered before she even had a chance to weigh in. While she didn't yet know who or what had turned Samantha against her parents, Megan believed that Joe and Lindy were completely sincere in their desire to do whatever it took to ensure their daughter's well-being.

They were willing to pay whatever it took. For Samantha's services, Danny's expertise and any other expense caring for their daughter would incur. They'd spare nothing for the best for their child.

Megan got that feeling in a whole new way as she waited for Danny to gas up the car to head back to Milwaukee. He'd fly out later that day, she was sure, but they had to talk first.

And suddenly, what she wanted, needed, felt, didn't matter a whit when compared to the well-being of the new life she carried.

A jolt passed through her as the thought of her new status took hold again. She was pregnant.

She was pregnant!

Vacillating between an inner sense of knowing, of acceptance, and shock at the reality of the life-changing news, she let it all wash over her. Didn't judge, or decide, question or worry for those moments.

Taking on a new reality, most particularly one of such magnitude, was a process she had to allow herself. She knew that.

Sometimes knowing and doing were worlds apart.

And the humongous change she was experiencing wasn't just hers.

It was Danny's, too. They might be using her body for the event, but the result belonged equally to both of them. The responsibility for the result rested on each of them. She wasn't solely in control. Which meant that she couldn't solely design how her new future was going to look.

And, oh God, she was pregnant! With Danny Tremaine's baby. The thought was so preposterous she couldn't wrap her mind around it.

And her heart…was in such a mixed-up jumble from elation to deathly fear…that, for once in her life, she couldn't rely on it. She'd hardly slept all night, bouncing back and forth along the vast spectrum, and hadn't yet found a place to land.

"You haven't moved since I got out of the car," Danny said, causing her to jump as he opened the driver's door and climbed back inside. "At first I thought you were asleep."

"Just thinking." There was only one thing that would have her in such a daze and they both knew what that was.

"We need to talk."

"Yep."

He started the car. Pulled out onto the long country road that would take them most of the way back to Milwaukee.

"I assume you're planning to have it."

It. Their baby.

"Yes." That was a choice she had to make. She was sorry for him, his lack of say on that one, but she couldn't not have the baby...

"I approve."

Warmth flooded her, but surprisingly...not surprise.

Maybe she'd known he would want her to have the baby. Danny spent many of his days just like she did—seeing to the rights and health and happiness of children—as he dealt with their parents' woes. And sometimes, when someone hired him as a child's advocate, he got to directly serve only the child.

Yeah, he was the guy who wanted to be free forever to pursue the life he knew he could live without causing undo pain in his wake. But he was also... Danny. He cared deeply. About humanity.

About his friends.

About his parents, even though their behavior pained him.

"You'll need to get home to see your doctor," he said then. "I'd like to be present for that. And while we might not be able to work it out for me to be at every monthly visit, I'd like to know about them, to hear a report on them, and most definitely want to fly in for any that include monitor screens and heartbeat sounds."

He'd just come from a morning of hearing a fight for a father's prenatal rights. Was clearly personalizing some of it.

Good Lord, what was she going into?

She smiled though. Inside and out.

"You do realize that every appointment, past the first one or two, involve listening to the heartbeat, right?"

"No." He frowned. Glanced at her.

"The doctor listens with a stethoscope every appointment during the second and third trimester."

At a stop sign, he looked over, met her gaze. Sat there. Until someone honked behind him.

"This is going to take a lot out of you," he said.

"It's going to give a lot to me, too." She was only just beginning to comprehend—both sides of that. Talking with him made it all seem so much more tangible than it had been all night long, as she'd lain there, her hands cradling her flat stomach, imagining...

"I can't even begin to see that, yet," he told her. And then quickly added, "I intend to be a father to it, you know."

She'd hoped. Hadn't been able to think about him, or his involvement, much.

"It's all just so weird."

"How so?"

"Well...it's you, you know?"

His glance that time was brief. She couldn't read him. Didn't know what to expect.

"I don't know you as a father."

"You can't see me as one, you mean."

"Maybe." He was Danny. And yet... "I know you'll make a great dad."

"It's okay, Meg. You don't need to spare my feelings." The odd tone of voice alerted her, and as she quickly replayed their conversation, her stomach sank. She'd hurt him.

"I'm not placating you, Danny. I've always known you would make a great father. In a way, you're like a father all day long, every day. Looking at the needs of others, giving your all to meeting those needs to the best of your ability. You assess all angles, try to find the best way to protect others' rights, to help them be happy. And isn't that, really, what parenting is all about?"

His shrug could have been a blow off, but she knew it wasn't. The truth ringing in her words had hit home—at least a little.

"You said something earlier this morning about never having said you didn't want to be a father, and you're right, you never did say that. But me thinking that you didn't want to be…that wasn't just about you not getting married. To be a father…you'd have one woman in your life who'd remain in your life, right? You'd be committed with her to raising the child. And it's that one woman, the same woman, commitment that you've always known you didn't want."

She wasn't really sure where she was going with the statement, but thoughts were there, behind the surface. Peeping through. Maybe…

…she was grasping at straws.

"Maybe I'm the perfect woman to give you the chance to be a father," she said anyway. "I know you, Danny. I have no expectation of fidelity, at least not in a man-woman sense. We aren't a couple and have no desire to be one because we have too much at stake that we both value way too much. But I know your heart. It's golden. I trust you implicitly to be the best father a child could have."

The truth rang like cathedral chimes inside her.

He glanced her way again. "There's no other woman I'd rather have as the mother of my child," he said. And then, when she started to panic as the thickness in the air between them got heavier, he said, "And Lord knows, I've known a lot of women."

She breathed. Grinned. And said, "Lord also knows that I obsess way too much about fidelity, so my chances of finding a guy that I can actually let myself love enough to marry are about nil," she added. "Look at Kurt. He was a great guy. And, as it turns out, he was faithful to me until the night we broke up. Yeah, it would have been nice if he'd timed it a little differently, you know the breakup, then the sex, but…" She shrugged. "I didn't open myself up to believing enough in our love to be able to trust him to be faithful…"

"Do not tell me that you're going to let this… change in your life…kill your dream of getting married and having the family you always wanted," Danny said, his tone serious again. "Lots of single mothers with fathers still in the picture get married, raise families."

Didn't she know it. She counseled children from blended families on a regular basis. But probably no more than children from two biological parent families.

Still…

She couldn't imagine…

Of course, she couldn't. She'd just found out she was pregnant with her best friend's child. How in the hell could she, why in the hell *would* she, bring another man and other children into the picture at that moment?

She might understand a lot of different people and circumstances, but in her personal life, she was only one woman.

"Give me a break, Tremaine." The words burst out of her. "I'm busy having my best friend's baby, at the moment. Really not in a mood to be dealing with an unknown man and wedding plans."

"Probably for the best," Danny said in his most irritating, tongue-in-cheek voice. "Because, you know, the whole reason you aren't married to Kurt is because your deepest self, you know the one you keep trying to get others to find, is really in love with me."

"Yeah, right," she scoffed.

"Not your fault really," he said. "I mean—" he ran his hand from in front of his face down his body "—look at this. Who could blame you?"

She shook her head. There was the best friend she'd known and loved for years. "I figured you out long ago, and while I'm grateful for the offer, I think I'll pass."

With a grin, he asked if she wanted to stop for something to eat.

She agreed.

And they went on about the business of getting through the next moments of the next days of a life they were only starting to see.

But as she sat across from him in yet another restaurant, perusing another menu, she couldn't quite shake what he'd said.

Did she really measure every other man against Danny?

Not sexually, certainly, as she'd never known

Danny that way when she'd dated, but was there some truth in what he said?

Was her friendship with him so deep, so close, that she hadn't left room for the love of her life to find her? Had she not given herself the chance to go find him?

It was definitely something to think about.

Once she got through with having a baby and figuring out how to be a single mother to Danny's child.

Danny was in three states over the next three days, consumed with work, on purpose. Each morning he'd text Meg, just to make sure…well…whatever, and then tell himself he wouldn't bother again until the next morning.

And each night, in his hotel room, picturing her alone in Milwaukee, with only a few hours of her day spent on the case, and loads of time to worry about the future, he'd end up calling her.

She was kind enough not to point out that he was being weird, phoning her every night.

In his better moments, he allowed himself to believe that he was helping. That his calls were giving her needed support. Letting her know that while she was going to be a single mother, she wasn't going it alone.

They talked about finances the first night. He'd brought up the topic after spending a flight from Wisconsin to Idaho, thinking about the legalities necessary to protect both Meg and the baby, to provide for them both for life, even if he were to die young.

He was taking out a hefty life insurance plan, for starters.

She'd argued. He'd been adamant.

She'd told him he was a jerk, in the teasing tone she reserved only for him, her way of accepting his decision.

He'd reminded her she loved him anyway.

And hung up smiling.

She'd told him, repeatedly, that she felt fine, perfectly normal, had had no further instances of nausea, but was staying away from fishy smells.

On the third night, he called from his condo in Denver. Samantha's ultrasound was the next day, and he wanted an update on the young woman's progress.

"She's been talking more," Megan told him. "Reliving memories of her childhood. She'll laugh, and then suddenly clam up."

"Something's going on."

"Yeah. And Carter exacerbates it. I'm just not sure that he or his mother is masterminding the whole thing."

"Who else would be? She's a happy, well-adjusted young woman until a couple of months after she starts dating the kid, and then, suddenly, she's happy with him and his mom, but not her own family?" Frustration didn't set well on him.

And neither did not being able to solve all the problems.

"Sammie and Carter, with Bella's help, have worked up an entire plan for their future. One that includes higher education for both of them. Bella's told them that they can stay with her, rent free, until one or the other of them is out of college, and she'll help with childcare. Once they're eighteen and married, they can get on public assistance for the baby's health care. And they plan to alternate class schedules, including taking night classes wherever possible, so that one or the other of them can be with the baby as much as possible. Both of them also plan to take part-time jobs."

"It's a big order."

"And possible for them to make it work. If they want it badly enough."

"And in four years, she's rich, so, really, who couldn't sacrifice like that for a few years if you knew the bounty was waiting?" He heard the sarcasm in his voice, wouldn't have let it fly with anyone but Meg. But…he was going to have a kid of his own, maybe even a daughter, and he sure as hell didn't want to go through the hell the Eversons were facing.

"I'm not saying there isn't a problem, Danny." Her tone, particularly serious, slowed him down.

"I know."

They both knew. The tension wasn't all because of the case. Most of it wasn't.

Stretched out on his couch, clothed in just the

gym shorts he'd pulled on after a shower to get rid of the travel grime, he thought about turning on a light, but was too tired to bother. He stared out the wall of windows, at the lights twinkling all over the city, and wondered why he'd never felt lonely in the place before.

Didn't like that he was feeling that way then.

"You tell your parents yet?" he asked.

"No. Have you?"

"Hell, no."

"Probably best to wait until we've figured things out and have answers to all of the questions they're going to throw at us."

"Your folks will gently lob. Mine will throw fast pitch." What now, he was feeling sorry for himself? Really not liking parts of himself all that much lately.

"Have you told anyone?" Her question came softly, with a vulnerable note that brought out every protective nerve in his body. She knew a part of her most private, personal business was his to give to whoever he chose.

"No. Have you?"

"It's not uncommon to wait until after the first trimester. Miscarriages are most common during the first three months…"

Miscarriage. Hadn't even entered his mind. He didn't go around thinking about dying in car accidents, either, though they did happen. Tense, he sat up.

"You having problems?" His heart pounded in his

chest. He thought about flight times to Wisconsin. He had the schedule memorized.

"No. Just being practical. And buying myself some time. I won't be showing until at least the fourth month, so it's not like anyone would figure it out. Maybe it's selfish, but I'd really like it if we could just keep this to ourselves for the moment. Just until I've had time to get used to it all."

"It's not selfish. It's smart. Emotionally and mentally healthy. As usual, coming from you. And I concur. Completely." He was lying down again, wondering if she was in her pajamas yet.

Wondering why he was getting hard pretty much every time he thought of her pregnant with his baby. Thought of her pajamas.

Or a smile on her face.

Obviously, the pregnancy was giving her a new potency that was making it more challenging for time to dissipate the effect of his sexual knowledge of her.

What was one more complication added to the list?

And what choice did he have but to deal with them all? He sure as hell wasn't walking away.

"I've been thinking a bit about afterward," he said, then. Trying to picture himself being a dad, was more like it. Trying to figure out where he'd fit in the kid's life. Would he be at birthday parties, for instance?

"I'm listening."

He'd known she would. Meg was great that way.

Always had been. Even before she'd become a therapist. "Maybe I sell my place here and buy a condo in Santa Barbara. Not right on top of you, of course. I'd find something a few miles away. Maybe even buy a house or a cottage or something on the beach."

"You love Colorado. You've always wanted to live there."

"Yeah, well, I like the ocean, too, and I want to live close enough to be included in birthday parties. And school pickups sometimes." When he was in town.

Or she was.

Oh, God. Sometimes he was such an ass. He hadn't even considered...

"What about your job, Meg? How are you going to travel?" And then he knocked the palm of his hand to his head, as he realized the selfishness of that remark. "No, wait. I can open a firm," he said. "Quit Sierra's Web and practice family law in one place..."

He didn't love the idea. But didn't think he hated it, either.

"No way are you leaving Sierra's Web," she said in a tone that said she clearly wasn't open to compromise on that one.

The final say was his, of course. But he liked her going to bat for him.

She always had, but with the baby...

They weren't a family. They were two adults with a child between them. A child's needs coming between them.

It wasn't just him and Meg anymore. Their relationship was changing.

And...

"I've already talked to Kelly about traveling less," Meg said, completely unaware of the depression he'd just splattered all over himself. "She didn't ask why, I didn't say, but it's likely she put it down to the breakup with Kurt and his marriage...anyway, she said it's not a problem. We get a lot of cases that can be handled virtually, and she'll send those my way. And I'll handle California, Arizona and Nevada cases—all areas where I can travel back and forth in a day. Flights to Phoenix are only forty-five minutes from Los Angeles. People commute far longer than that on LA freeways every day."

"If I'm based in California, too, I'll be able to take up slack when a case requires you to be gone a few days."

Clearly, they were going to be working less together.

He was losing her.

And gaining a child.

Despair and an odd kind of euphoria all rolled into one inside him.

Trapping him within a reality he couldn't change.

Leaving him with no clear path forward.

He had no idea how to live with a problem he couldn't fix.

Chapter Fourteen

Danny was going to move to California? Meg couldn't quite wrap her mind around the changes that he was going to make.

Not as many as a baby coming permanently to her life, of course, but...wow.

They could meet for drinks every now and then. After she had the baby of course.

She'd be able to see him more frequently.

And...they wouldn't be spending nights on the road, isolated from the world, with adjoining doors open between them in hotel rooms.

Not often, anyway.

She'd thought that no matter what happened in their personal lives—even her marriage to Kurt—nothing would ever change her life with Danny.

At least not until they were old and gray and maybe started to think about retiring. A concept so far into the future that it didn't feel real.

Having a baby growing inside her—his baby— didn't feel real, either.

The change was so instant, and so all-consuming…she didn't feel like herself.

And it hit her, the morning after Danny had told her he was moving to California, that she'd been missing the absolute obvious with the case. Samantha was having a hard time being herself because… she wasn't that self anymore.

She was pregnant. Going to be a mother. She couldn't go back to being her parents' little girl anymore.

Of course, they weren't expecting her to be.

But what if Samantha hadn't let herself see that yet? What if a part of her didn't want to let go of that little girl yet?

She'd just turned seventeen, was getting ready to start her senior year in high school. A time when there'd have been a lot of celebrations as her school community, her parents, celebrated her last official year of childhood and induction into adulthood.

What if she was taking out on her parents the anger she felt for the things her pregnancy had stolen from her? Things she really wanted.

She'd been watching Samantha's relationship with the Wilsons, observing for signs of manipulation and brainwashing, and working hard to build trust with Samantha. She'd been analyzing everything the young woman said for signs of mental or emotional abuse...but what if the answers were simpler, and in a way more complicated, than that?

The theory didn't completely track...if Samantha's hostility was based solely on what had been robbed from her, she'd likely be resistant to Bella's attempts to give her so much less than she'd previously had. And she'd likely be angry with Carter, too, fairly or not, as he was the one who'd robbed her by making her pregnant. Megan didn't hold Carter any more responsible for the pregnancy than she did Samantha, if the sex was consensual and sought equally by both parties. They'd be equally responsible. But a normal reaction for a seventeen-year-old would be to place blame on the party that caused the result.

But so far, Megan was unsure that the sex had been equally sought and completely consensual. Samantha wouldn't talk about the baby's conception.

Or sex, period. With Carter or anyone.

But she didn't exhibit any kind of fear of the young man. To the contrary, she seemed to find strength in her communication with him.

Carter, for his part, had fulfilled all requirements of the signed and resigned decree, and appeared to be encouraging Samantha to do so as well.

But then, why wouldn't he? He didn't want to face a possible restraining order fight.

Nor would he want to risk any chance he had of benefiting from Sammie's trust fund or inheritance, if the money was his true motive.

Frustrated, Megan sat at the table in her hotel room, dressed in a brown cotton skirt, peasant top and brown sandals, glancing out the window at the busy city street below. She'd planned to spend her morning reading. Perhaps the wiser choice would have been to go for a walk. Immerse herself in the bustling lives of others, clear her mind.

She'd finished her breakfast and had an hour until lunch, then another hour to get to Blaine for her last meeting with Samantha before the appointment with the ultrasound technician late that afternoon—scheduled for when Carter got off work.

Megan wouldn't be going to that appointment. She had a late afternoon video conference with Kelly to discuss upcoming caseloads, and hopefully, would get some new assignments immediately that could be handled virtually. All of the downtime in Milwaukee wasn't healthy for her.

Her thoughts jumped from her own personal situation—a topic she was trying to avoid during the workday—back to Samantha.

The only people Samantha appeared hostile toward were her parents. Did she somehow blame them for not protecting her from pregnancy? For allowing her to go out with a boy who'd tempt her to the point of unprotected sex?

For not knowing that she'd been struggling with the temptation?

Again, didn't fully track, as Samantha relayed wonderful stories of times with her parents—as recently as five months before. All hostility was absent during those conversations.

The only thing she knew for certain was that Samantha Everson was exhibiting anger and resentment for a reason.

Because she was pregnant? How long before she'd announced her state and left home had she known that she was going to have a baby? Because the signs of hostility had begun prior to that day.

Megan knew the date of the hCG test conducted at the free clinic in Milwaukee. But Samantha obviously had had a concern before that date, or she wouldn't have been there.

The questions had been asked, gently, more than once, during the session Megan held with Samantha, but the girl either didn't answer at all, or just shrugged and said she wasn't sure.

Clearly withholding.

And the huge unanswered question hanging over Megan was "why."

Sammie's anger seemed to be stemming from pregnancy. Obviously, there'd be situations that would cause the reaction. The unexpectedness of it, certainly, if one's life was completely upended by the unplanned event, could be a stimulator.

As she had the thought, a mental picture of Danny's smiling face popped up. Filling her mind. And her heart.

Danny was probably the most genuine human being she'd ever known.

Honest with himself and others. To the point of abiding, always, by the guidelines with which he lived, taking accountability for his actions, even when it meant denying himself the security or companionship of a full-time partner.

He was honest enough to admit he didn't want a full-time partner.

And there he was, in spite of everything, his openness, trapped for life. They didn't have to be married, or even speak all that often, but they'd be forever tied, partners for life, in the raising of their offspring.

The warm glow that shot through her was better than the orgasm Danny had given her.

And left a shard of fear in her heart, as well.

While she wouldn't have chosen to be pregnant with Danny's baby in a million years, she couldn't find the least bit of anger inside her.

Fear…yeah, there was a fair amount of that.

Regret…a big hell yeah, there.

But anger?

She shook her head. And thought of Danny, again.

Was he angry? He had reason to be.

A right to be—even if just angry with himself.

Or angry with fate for a life thrown irreparably off course.

Buried anger boded nothing good. To the contrary, it could lead to major problems down the road that would disrupt not only Danny's life, but his child's too, without him even knowing why.

He'd start to make bad choices, little things at first, probably, and then get angry at the consequences. If he didn't seek help, things could stoneroll from there...

Even while she knew that she was being overdramatic, failing to take into account Danny's personality and lifetime of self-control, she picked up the phone.

He answered on the first ring.

"Hey, what's up?"

"You still at home?"

"For another hour, yes. Then I'm heading to Chicago, meeting Savannah for an emergency consult late this afternoon. What's up?"

Savannah Raleigh—the Sierra's Web partner who headed up the firm's law team. One of the seven college friends, Kelly included, who'd started the firm over a decade ago.

A beautiful single woman.

Had that just been a bolt of jealousy passing through her? Seriously?

She was not going to do that. Danny was no more hers at that moment than he'd ever been. She'd never lost sleep over the women in his life. And Savannah and Danny both were ultimate professionals.

"Meg? Everything okay?" His tone had sharpened, and she stood at the window, shaking her head. Too much time in the room by herself.

With too much out of her control weighing on her mind.

"Yes, of course," she said, but then continued. "I was thinking about Samantha's hostility, looking at sources for the anger, and it occurred to me that unexpected pregnancy, the life altering changes it forced, as a contributor, could be far-reaching if not acknowledged."

"Are we talking about Samantha here?"

"No."

Silence hung on the line. Too long. "Danny?"

"You called to tell me you're angry," he finally said. "I'm searching for a suitable response."

She didn't want suitable. She needed honesty. "You can stop searching," she said. "I'm not angry. Maybe I should be, but I find that I am not."

"So why the ca…oh, I get it, you think I'm angry."

"I think that you have reason to be, and that if you are, we need to address it right away so that it doesn't bore down in and fester."

"You're playing shrink on me."

"Maybe. And friend. And expectant mother of your child. This whole thing is fraught with so much baggage, Danny, so many ways for us to trip up, and the only way we give our child the secure happy love-filled life we both want it to have, is to keep our eyes wide open every step of the way."

The sound that came over the line offended her...

"Are you laughing at me right now?"

Chuckling was more like it, not an all-out guffaw. Her reaction was the same. A slam in the chest. Hurt.

Danny never hurt her.

"I'm not laughing at you," he said, sounding wearier than amused then. "I'm chuckling at the absurdity of this situation. You and I have never talked about what kind of life we'd want to give any child either of us might have, and yet...you know exactly."

Frowning, she waited. "Was I wrong?"

"No! That's the whole point. You just knew."

"We've talked a lot about our childhoods over the years. Commiserated." She was smiling, then, too. Thinking of him in his condo. Picturing his steady, rock-solid shoulders in shirt and suit jacket, ready for travel. Wishing he was on his way to her. "This really is about as weird as it gets, isn't it?"

"A bit."

"So...are you angry, Danny?"

"Strangely enough, no. I wish things were different. I wish to hell it hadn't happened. I'm concerned about the future. Frustrated. Regretful. Sad, even. But...not angry."

She was all those things, too. And more. Elated, topping the list. She was carrying the baby of the man she considered one of the most special individuals on earth. Her soul mate.

But then, she didn't have an active sex life to contend with. To compete with or complicate the whole idea of carrying a child.

"I just want you to know…your regular personal life, you know, socializing, the women… I have absolutely no expectation for that to change, Danny. That's a part of you separate and apart from me, and I'm good with that. I don't want there to be any misunderstandings or false impressions. No reason for you to put pressure where there is none, or create tension based on misinformation."

Lust would fade. They'd starve it to death, and it would shrivel up and die as though it had never been.

That was the plan.

And the only way their bizarre situation had a hope of working.

"Thank you for that. For bringing it up. Though, it hasn't been my top priority at the moment, it's good to know for the future."

Okay, then. Well, good. It would be good, anyway. In the future. But there was something else on her mind.

"When I asked you not to say anything to anyone about this yet, to give me a chance to acclimate, I wasn't considering that there might actually be a current companion in your life. And that if that's the case, I can't reasonably expect you not to say something if you so choose."

Danny didn't commit long term, but he was always monogamous during the time he was seeing someone.

He cleared his throat. As he did often before beginning to argue a case to a judge. She'd always thought it was a tell of his, signaling that he was drawing himself into acute focus.

"First, the whole point of noncommitted relationships is that matters of a personal, or intensely emotional manner, are not shared. It is by so sharing that relationships grow into a depth that creates space for severely hurt feelings."

She almost smiled. Blinked back the tears in her eyes.

That which he didn't allow in his sexual encounters, he'd been sharing with her for over a decade. In the midst of all of their barbing back and forth. Their bets and challenges. Their debates and social conversations. They talked about matters of a personal or intensely emotional manner.

"And second," he continued while she dealt with her silent emotional blabbering, "I've actually only had one intimate companion in over a year. Two, including the night that shall not be discussed again."

Two, including her.

"Wow," she said, actually frowning in concern, while her insides bubbled with a spring of something akin to pleasure. The concern quickly won out. "Why? Are you okay?"

There had certainly been nothing at all wrong with his working parts the night he'd left his baby seed inside her.

"Growing up, I'm afraid," he said with a modicum of regret. "My idea of sexy these days is having my toothbrush where I sleep. Just more convenient, you know. And having my lover's toothbrush there, too. Morning breath and all."

Heart stopping, she could barely hold the phone. Was Danny actually ready to settle down? Could it be…

Not for them. Trying to make more of them, bringing in the expectation, the jealousy…and it would be there, based on the bout of it she'd experienced in this very phone call…it would ruin them.

But still, it complicated matters. It meant her child was going to have a stepmom someday. She'd not only be sharing Danny, but her child, too.

"Problem is, the toothbrush being there doesn't mean I want to move to a deeper level. I only want it there until the joy of seeing those toothbrushes together fades. And it's not as easy finding a woman who gets that, as it was finding one who understood no commitment."

"Toothbrushes together does send a bit of a different message," she admitted, riding her roller coaster emotions as best she could.

"Yeah, so how about you? I know you joked about being too busy birthing a baby in the upcoming months to explore romantic possibilities, but are there any Kurt replacers on the horizon?"

"Still not thinking I'll have any leftover energy to go hunting over the next nine months."

"I actually meant someone already in the picture." Was that insecurity she heard in his voice? Vulnerability?

About her romantic life? She struggled to wrap her mind around that change.

"You think you wouldn't have heard? You know I always run Mr. Right by you." And by her definition, that meant any guy she dated more than casually.

"So, to sum up…we're both pathetic. I will date as usual, you won't be dating, and neither of us is angry. You good with that, Doctor?"

Shaking her head, she gave him a dirty look he couldn't see. "Yes, Counselor."

"Good, can I go now? I have a plane to catch."

She thought about hanging up on him. Hadn't done it in a while.

"Fly safe," she said instead.

To which he replied, "Good luck with Samantha."

And they both hung up.

There was no measurable reason for her step to be lighter, or her nervous energy to be calmed, but there it was.

A phone call with Danny, and she was herself again. Ready to go to work.

Even while everything about her was changing. From the inside out.

Chapter Fifteen

Coming out of his meeting with Savannah late that afternoon, Danny checked the phone that had been vibrating against his chest for the past ten minutes.

Joe Everson. Three times.

Less than a minute after returning the call, he had to excuse himself from his work with Savannah. He had to get to Milwaukee. The Eversons were at the end of their patience, and they wanted to take action. He'd even briefly spoken with Meg. She'd be at the hotel, waiting for him when he got there.

Savannah offered to drive him herself, saying it could give them time to finish their work together, and he gratefully accepted.

Savannah had requested his opinion before she proceeded with her next, complicated case. It involved a defendant who'd used his minor child to build trust in his victims. Savannah's client, the defendant's wife, who was under investigation as well, claimed complete innocence and was relying on Savannah to help her prove as much. She also wanted custodial rights of her child. But should Savannah pursue that now?

After meeting with the wife and watching an earlier interview with the precocious four-year-old boy, Danny was more inclined to put the mother's character on the line without the child's testimony. Anything the boy might say were just words. A mother fighting to bring her son home, to love and care for him, was action.

By the time she dropped him at the hotel in Milwaukee, she'd agreed with his opinion. She'd wait to look over all discoveries that had been ordered, and then decide whether or not to proceed.

She wished him luck on his case—knowing how much Meg was opposed to what the Eversons wanted to do—and didn't even turn off the car as he climbed out, grabbing his overnight bag off the back seat.

Yeah, Meg wasn't going to be happy with the decision that had already been made. She'd try like hell to talk to him out of it. Or rather, to find a better solution, but the Eversons were done listening.

However, his and Meg's differing professional positions wasn't the biggest problem he faced as he walked into the hotel lobby and saw Meg waiting for him, the lone person in an upholstered furniture living room type conversation area off to the left of reception.

His boss didn't know he'd gotten his coworker pregnant in that very hotel a few weeks before.

And she most certainly didn't know how badly he'd wanted an excuse to make the quick jaunt from Chicago to Milwaukee to see her after his session with Savannah.

Not at the expense of the Eversons, ever.

And yet, because of them, there he was.

And there she was, in an above the knee skirt, peasant top, and that blond flyaway hair that made him hard…

What the hell.

Leaving his bag with the bellman, asking to have it delivered to his room, adjacent to Meg's, he invited her to dinner. She was feeding two. She had to eat.

She accepted. And as they were walking toward the pub, asked, "Was that Savannah dropping you off?"

"Yes."

"Why didn't she come in?"

"She had to get back. Start going through discovery before another meeting with her client in the morning."

"Nice of her to take the time to drive you up." But Meg didn't sound nice. She sounded crotchety.

"She needed another hour of my time."

And why did he suddenly feel as though he was under an inquisition? Or had to defend himself? His mode of transportation, or anything else that she might dig at him about.

Was she really going to be pissy with him for doing his job?

His client had every right to prevent a person/or people they thought were hurting their daughter from getting within twenty feet of her, and, most importantly, preventing them from communicating with her in any fashion or by any means.

Meg knew the score.

And didn't say any more until they were seated. Yet another booth. One they hadn't yet been in together. And were waited on by a waitress they'd never seen. He ordered the pepper steak as soon as she arrived, with tea. Meg wanted an oriental chicken salad and decaffeinated coffee.

Hot coffee at night.

Everything was changing.

She hadn't looked at him. Other than ordering, she hadn't said anything.

He was starting to feel a bit peeved, too.

"I'm sorry."

His gaze shot to hers as soon as he heard the tone of voice. Meg was back.

"For what?" He frowned. "More to the point, what did I do to piss you off?"

"I can't believe I'm saying this, but...for a second or two today, I've been jealous of Savannah."

"Jealous?" He was at a complete loss, hearing those words coming from his best friend. They didn't even compute. "Whatever for? She and I have worked cases several times."

And it had never had a bearing on his friendship with Meg. She couldn't possibly be upset that he worked with other female experts at the firm. She worked with other male experts, too. They always had.

"Are you saying you don't want me to associate with other women?"

"No! Of course not. You know me better than that."

"You can't help how you feel." He'd heard the phrase from her often enough over the years. *You can't help how you feel, but you can help what you do with or about those feelings.*

"It's not how I feel."

"You want me to stop having sexual associations for a while?" The idea didn't bother him a whit. Other women were the last thing on his mind.

"Of course not."

And...the pleading look she shot him shut up his mental tirade. "Talk to me."

"I just...feel like I'm losing you. Or losing what made us *us*. I can't understand it myself, so there's no way I can explain it. I just want you to know I'm aware, and that I'll fix it."

That he got. Smiled a purposefully killer smile. Because...she was his Meg.

They were "them." Talking things through was what they did. What made "them" work.

"Is it too early for the hormonal mood swings?" he asked, not lightly, but wishing he could take some of the weight from her.

"Probably."

He nodded. Smiled again. Was all puffed up when she smiled back.

"Let's go easy on ourselves for a little bit, okay?" he asked then. Pleading for some leeway for himself as much as her. "This is huge. And sudden. We're going to feel things foreign to us. But as long as we talk about it—" as he had his sexual attraction to her "—we'll get through it together."

He was beginning to sound like some kind of therapist himself. He'd learned a lot from her over the years.

Her grin that time was genuine. Filled her face, her eyes. Lit him up in ways it shouldn't have...

"I love ya," she said flippantly, but, again, that was "them."

"Back at ya."

They had to talk about the case. But he needed a moment.

Time to be with his friend and feel...okay.

Mostly, to make sure she was okay.

Then they'd be ready to take on the world again.

Together.

And alone, too.

Because that was how they rolled.

They had to talk about the case. Talking upstairs was out. No way she should be alone with Danny in a hotel room, any hotel room, let alone one that looked exactly like the one they'd done the deed in.

There was some science to the fact that women's sexual drive amped up during pregnancy, but not in the first month.

No, more likely, it was what so many women had known before her—sex with Danny was addictive. There was nothing else like it on earth.

"Let's go down to the Riverwalk," she blurted as he signed the bill to his tab. They'd eaten. And absolutely were not drinking.

No valid reason to continue to take up a seat that could earn a hardworking waitress more tips.

And she needed out. Fresh air. Space from Danny while staying close to him.

Just steps from the hotel, they joined other walkers, mostly vacationers, she figured, as they strolled along the three-sectioned paved way along the Milwaukee River, crossing over bronze medallions, river inspired artwork from elementary-school-aged children that had been set in bronze. She hadn't known they were there. Hadn't ever heard of anything like them. And couldn't help wondering if her and Danny's baby would be artistic...

One minute they were talking about art. Historic buildings. The surprising cleanliness of the river water floating beside them.

And then she'd been consumed with thoughts of their baby.

Wanted to take his hand and be a couple like so many they were passing...

They had to talk about the case. It was why they were there.

"At her last appointment, Samantha was lying on a table, feeling exposed, with everyone looming over and around her, and was pushed into an emotional corner from which she couldn't escape. Fight or flight instincts kicked in and she fought. Which is what we want, by the way." Out of the blue, she just started laying out the facts that she needed Danny to understand so that they could figure out a way to prevent the explosion that he was about to detonate.

Her own fight or flight instincts had kicked in, leaving her no choice but to fight off the inappropriate emotions assailing her and get to work.

"We need for her to be fighting her way out of whatever it is that's making her so angry, most particularly if she's being manipulated," she reminded him. "If she's in the process of taking back her own mind, which has been what we're working toward, then these weeks of work are going to be for naught, her progress will be jeopardized, if they file that restraining order. We could lose her."

"Carter is the one who pushed her into that corner, Meg. Joe and Lindy watched it happen."

"The way she told it, Lindy was at the side of the table the whole time, talking to the technician, watching everything…"

"Isn't that what mothers of pregnant teens do? Look out for their daughters? Knowing what's going on, what's coming, and with her responsibility to her daughter, Lindy was being observant. No more."

Megan, looking up at a particularly beautiful historical building, reminded herself she wasn't fighting Danny. Not professionally, and not personally, either.

She needed his understanding, though. More then than ever. Personally, probably more than professionally. She couldn't let his nearness, her hunger for more intimate closeness, her new vulnerability, affect the job they were doing.

"She didn't move to let Carter be next to Samantha when they were searching for the heartbeat."

"According to Joe, Samantha didn't even notice. She was too busy watching the monitor. Carter is the one who made the issue, Meg. He demanded that the procedure be stopped. And when everyone in the room, including the technician, turned eyes on him, he pushed past Lindy right next to Samantha."

"The mother of his child. I agree, he shouldn't

have pushed past Lindy. Clearly emotions were running high. He was already upset that Bella hadn't been able to come into the room."

"There was a limit to how many people could be there. It would have been better had they known that ahead of time, I agree, but it was what it was."

"I know, but Samantha had a valid point, Danny. Both of her parents were there, but Danny couldn't have one? Bella's a mother, too. Joe could have waited outside and let Bella have his space."

"Joe and Lindy are responsible for their daughter, and her unborn child, until Samantha turns eighteen. And they're concerned about the change that has come over her since Carter came into her life. It's understandable that they feel a need to stand guard, so to speak."

"And that's exactly how she feels. As though they're standing guard, her prison wardens, not her parents."

"You know that's not fair."

"Not from our perspective, of course not, but we're dealing with the standpoint of a troubled, unexpectedly pregnant, seventeen-year-old girl. If we aren't going to give credence to her views, why am I even here?"

"We've been doing little else, Meg. For weeks now. Carter physically moved Lindy's body with his own. He pushed her..."

"Samantha agreed that he shouldn't have moved

her mother, but there was only enough pressure to get by her, not to shove or in any way be aggressive against her."

"Joe doesn't see it that way. He witnessed the young man shoving his wife out of the way of his daughter. We aren't going to get him to go back on that one. The minute Carter laid hands on Lindy Everson, Joe was done. And Lindy…maybe she could have gotten around the push…maybe…but when Carter stood over Samantha, looking her straight in the eye, and demanded that she choose who got to be there, him or her mother…that's when we lost Lindy's support. Again, they still want you to work with Samantha. They believe you're her only hope…"

She already knew that. Joe had called her on his way home from the clinic. Samantha had insisted on riding back to the house with Carter.

The young woman had called her, too. Later.

"But they also have to do what they feel is right to protect Samantha in the meantime," Danny continued. "They can't just sit back and leave all of the work to you when their instincts are telling them that they need to act before it's too late."

"Or are they knee-jerk reacting because their daughter chose Carter? Which, under any of the scenarios we're theorizing in our attempt to figure out what's really going on inside her, she would feel forced to do. Even if it's just that she's desperately in love with the father of her child."

In love with the father of her child. The words hung like tangible points in the air in front of her face. Had Danny noticed?

She loved him.

She wasn't *in love* with him.

The significance of that could be the difference between life and death for them.

What that particular significance was, how she defined the difference, was something she was going to have to look at.

When Samantha was cared for and Megan was alone.

"He was wrong to make her choose."

"He's a kid."

"She screamed at her parents to get out of the room."

"Because Joe moved forward, she was afraid he was going to make Carter leave."

"Has Joe ever grabbed anyone in anger? Ever in his life?"

"There's been no indication of or witness to that."

"Did you ask Samantha if she was afraid of her father, physically? If he had exhibited violent tendencies?"

"Of course, several times over the course of the past weeks."

"And?"

"You know the answer to that, Danny. Just as I know that the technician also said that there was nothing physically menacing about Joe approaching the exam table. Samantha, believe it or not, also told me that she didn't fear that her father was going to hurt anyone. She just thought he was going to start a verbal fight with Carter. Yell at him, were her exact words. That's what pushed her into the emotional corner, and why she yelled, first."

They were getting nowhere. He wasn't open to finding another solution.

And maybe she wasn't, either. She needed it her way. He needed it his.

He might as well have already filed the motion, it was that much of a done deal.

No magic to be found between her and Danny that night.

They'd walked nearly a mile from their hotel. "You want to head back?" she asked, turning around as he nodded.

They walked in silence for the next five minutes. Megan didn't even want to guess what Danny was thinking. And wasn't all that fond of tuning into her own thoughts, either.

People milled around, some in suits, like Danny, probably in town on business. She'd chosen her skirt and top in deference to her meeting with Samantha earlier that morning.

A time seemingly so distant, she could hardly believe they were in the same day.

"We actually made some progress this morning,"

she said, with much less agitation driving her words. Just talking. Not fighting for anything. "Samantha started talking about seeing herself differently. She asked me what you did when you didn't like what you saw." There was more that she didn't feel comfortable sharing—though it was legal that she do so. With Danny.

But that…

"It reminded me of…"

"I know, me. In college. I didn't want to be known as the heartbreaker."

That was really what had started it all. Their friendship. For her at least. The fact that he'd cared about the hearts getting broken. And that he'd been willing to change some things about himself, to be more honest with the various women in his life, to prevent causing any more pain.

Her heart lurched. Definitely pain there.

Not anything she had any iention of sharing. Ever.

"Samantha's most definitely in crisis. Warring inside herself. I just can't yet determine who's the general in the battle. Or what the fight is specifically about. What started it. I need more time."

Joe and Lindy Everson had assured her she'd have all the time she needed.

They didn't seem to get that no amount of time was going to help if Samantha's ability to be open got buried so deeply in their avalanche that it suffocated and died…

"You'll have a few more days, Meg, before the matter of the final order is brought before the judge, before a decision is made."

"But, even if only temporary, the orders go into effect immediately, until the judge makes a final decision. There'd still be the possibility that it won't be finalized and won't go on his record, but there will be no more contact."

She couldn't imagine…being told she could never see or talk to Danny, to the father of her baby…

She was thirty-one. A capable adult with life experience. Not to be compared with a lost seventeen-year-old.

But the concept of being denied contact with someone you believed would be your partner for life…even if you didn't fully comprehend what that meant…being pregnant so young and having to choose between those you loved, between your support systems, while you had a dependent little one coming to life inside you.

Despair filled her and she shook her head. She couldn't save Samantha from the pain her life might bring her. She could only help her be as mentally and emotionally healthy as possible, and hopefully give her coping skills that would see her through.

And she might lose that chance, too. She could very well lose Samantha's trust. The young woman wasn't going to be given a heads-up about the restraining order being filed until after the immediate, temporary order had been put in place. Her father didn't want her to tip off Carter. Her mother feared the young couple might try to run before law enforcement was able to serve the order. They wanted Megan to be present when Samantha found out.

"I don't think I should be there when they tell her," she said as they drew nearer to their hotel. "I'll be in town, available, but if I'm in the room, it's going to look like I'm part of the group of adults who did this to her. To Carter and Bella."

"I understand."

He wasn't even trying to find a way for them to come together on this one. He had to follow his clients' requests, or quit the job. She understood that. She even comprehended the fact that Danny agreed with his clients, that he'd probably advised them that, as they'd determined, it was time. But never had there been a time when he wasn't open to finding another way.

"I think it might be good for you to be there, though," she told him. Things were so volatile with the little family...

"I intend to be the one to tell her, at her parents' request, of course."

A famous brewery came into view and they talked about it, about beer in general, about other buildings in the downtown area, and about what time they'd meet in the morning to head to Blaine, until they were on their floor, approaching the two doors behind which they were going to disappear. Separately.

He didn't stop at her door, continuing toward his. "Danny?"

He slowed, glanced back at her. "It's already happened, hasn't it?" she asked. "Us. We've changed."

With a side tilt of his head, he gave her hope for a second, led her to think he had a way to save them, still.

"Yeah," he said instead. "I think it has."

She went inside her room then, didn't listen for the closing of his door.

She was too busy fighting the tears she promised herself wouldn't fall.

But they did.

Chapter Sixteen

He had to fix it. Them. The problems. Everything. Danny wasn't the sort to sit around and deal with things. He was the guy who found solutions and implemented them.

The following evening, after a grueling day in Blaine, he sat across from Meg at dinner, talking about things he didn't give two hoots about at the moment, searching for the spark that always shot from her eyes to his soul.

She'd said they were soul mates and while he might never have had the thought in exactly that way, he knew she'd been exactly right. As she generally was when it came to matters of the heart and mind.

"Samantha seemed to be doing better by the time

we left," he said, mostly because she'd yet to engage with him that entire day.

Her body was present, her mind shared facts, but the Meg he knew was nowhere to be found.

"For now," she told him. She'd spent a couple of hours alone with the teenager that afternoon, following a horrible session in which Danny had told Samantha about the temporary restraining orders that had been granted that morning, against Bella and Carter. He'd explained that there would be a formal hearing set in six days, at which time, if the judge found cause, a permanent injunction would be filed and would be in effect until she was eighteen. That was after the baby was born.

What it meant: if Samantha contacted Carter at all, in any way, and he responded in any fashion, she would be leading him to his arrest. Danny had also explained that Carter would have his day in court and could argue for the permanent injunction to be denied. He'd also be permitted to argue his rights as a father-to-be at that time.

Samantha had remained silent, an expressionless statue, until he'd asked if she had any questions. She'd ranted. She'd screamed. Had thrown her new expensive phone toward her parents, shattering the screen. "Here, have it!" she'd said as the cell hit the corner of a table to the left of them.

And then she'd run upstairs and locked herself in her room, refusing to come out.

But half an hour later, she'd used the landline phone in her room to call Megan. And by the end of the afternoon, the two of them had returned with Samantha's damaged cell phone fixed, paid for out of her allowance.

Beyond that, Danny knew nothing.

"You ready to go up?" Meg motioned for the bill as she made a request that appeared to be completely rhetorical. She was going up whether he was ready or not.

"You planning to renege on our plans to co-parent a child?" he replied.

"Of course not. Don't be childish, Danny." And with that she stood, signed the tab that was on its way to them, and stood there waiting for him to stand and walk out with her.

They talked about schedules on their way upstairs, with Meg watching the floor indicator lights tick by up above the door. She'd be taking him to the airport in the morning, before heading back to Blaine. He'd be back in town the following week, unless there was cause for him to return earlier. The Eversons had extended their request for Meg's full-time employment at least through the following week. She'd accepted on the spot.

As soon as the elevator opened on their floor, Meg, key card already in hand, headed straight for her room, swiped the card, swung the door, called out a kind sounding "see you in the morning" and let the door swing shut.

He got it.

Figured she was making the transition they both had to make with much more aplomb and class than he'd shown.

And...what the hell.

They'd had sex once.

Sex. It came. It went.

It didn't get in the way.

Except it was getting in the way.

Because...

They were holding on to it. Letting it remain between them. Building a wall. One that could become impenetrable.

In the hall, he approached her door. Raised his hand to knock. Stepped back.

Entered his own room. Stewed for another half hour.

Listened for her. Heard nothing.

He was leaving in the morning.

And he didn't want to leave things so stilted between them. The distance was excruciating even standing feet away from her with only a wall, not several states, between them.

She was the relationship-wise one of the two of them. Taking her lead was the smart choice to make.

Unless, maybe, because she was hurting and confused, too, she couldn't see clearly. The thought took hold.

It led him to the adjoining door between their rooms. And before he could use his judgment to weigh the consequences of his actions, he knocked.

Firmly.

She'd changed into her pajamas. But then, apparently upon his knock, had pulled her clothes back on. The pajama bottoms were sticking out below the skirt.

Something slightly sarcastic about her unusual fashion statement was on the tip of his tongue. His lips were busy following his eyes to her mouth.

He kissed her. Right there. Right then. In the doorway between their rooms. His lips planted on hers, coaxing, encouraging, and when her lips parted, he did a little tongue dancing, too. Basic stuff that was always nice.

But something was wrong. Not at all usual. Exploding on him. Electricity. His tongue. Hers. Need.

Moans.

More.

"No!" Megan pulled back with such force his mouth stung.

Turning her back, she walked toward the window with the curtains still wide open to the lights of the city below, and in the distance.

"Cute look, Latimer." He said what he should have

said when she'd first opened the door. After what he'd just done, the effectiveness fell completely flat.

She turned, rubbing her mouth as she looked at him. "What are you doing, Danny?" Her gaze shadowed, dark, struck fear in him. Heart-thumping fear. She'd never looked at him like that before.

"Making an error in judgment," he guessed. "A huge one. Biggest ever." Shut up. Think.

And… "I'm sorry. If you want to file a complaint with Sierra's Web, I'll back you up. In fact, no way you have to do that. I'll quit. Right now." He pulled out his phone. "I'm quitting."

"Danny." One word. Filled with so much he didn't understand. He got it, though, when she took his phone.

He wasn't quitting yet.

He would have, though. If she hadn't stopped him. He'd probably be leaving the firm, anyway, to open a practice in Santa Barbara. No way was he going to be away for all of the important moments, and during unexpected crises, when his kid was growing up.

Could he take an eighteen-year leave of absence?

He'd kissed Megan.

"I'm sorry," he said again with a sigh, slumping down to one of the two chairs at the table in front of the window, looking out at a night that had just been witness to his stupidest move, ever.

"What are you doing?" she asked, pacing back and forth in her ridiculous garb.

The hastily donned peasant blouse covered the slit between top and bottoms, that little sliver of stomach. He still knew it was there.

Could clearly tell she wasn't wearing a bra.

Meg hated them. The tightness around her ribs all day long.

Just a tidbit he'd picked up along the way somewhere that chose to bother him at that particular point in time.

"Danny, talk to me."

There. That. Talk.

"That's what we do," he said. "Talk to each other. About anything and everything."

Whether it was his words, or his pathetic loser tone, he didn't know, but she joined him at the table. Crossing her arms over her double clothed breasts as she sat.

"Yeah." Her diction left something to be desired.

"We haven't been talking to each other. We've been—"

"Talking *at* each other, I know," she interrupted. "So, here we are. Talk. Starting with…what in the hell was that all about?" She pointed toward the adjoining door.

"You responded." It wasn't just him. That had to be the first topic.

"I'm aware."

"You liked it."

"And this is news, how? It's you. The great Danny Tremaine. Who wouldn't like it?"

Another day and time, say a decade earlier, he might have liked that comment.

"I liked it, too."

"That's not news, either. You enjoy sex, Danny."

He eyed her for a long moment. He might not have an advanced degree in psychiatry, might not be a medical doctor but he had a juris-doctorate. And a lawyer who couldn't assess people wasn't going to get very far. "You wanted it, too."

"Too as in I liked it *and* wanted it? Or too as in, *you* wanted it as well."

So like her to put it back on him. But then, he had started it. "Too as in I wanted it as well."

Her lips puckered as she nodded, like she was analyzing him, considering his response on some therapist scale of serious diagnoses.

Might have been more impressive to him if his dropped gaze hadn't just landed on the pajama pants sticking out from the bottom of her skirt.

Reminding him she wasn't in top form. That she was gifted in her field but she was human, too. A woman with a huge heart, and feelings and...

He had to fix things.

"The sex is in the way," he said, looking her right in the eye. Then shrugged. "What I know about sex—and as you've rightly pointed out, I'm a bit of an expert on the subject—is that if you let it take its course, it burns out. In my expert opinion, the way to get us back to being soul mates, best friends, and generally individuals who can talk to each other about pretty much anything, is to take care of the sex."

Her stilted nod might have made him smile if he was watching a movie. But it was Meg. And real life.

"Take care of the sex."

"Yeah." He nodded vigorously to show her that he was confident in his solution.

"How do you propose we do that?"

"By doing it so it can fade."

"I'm thinking time and not doing it is a better solution," she told him. "The more you do it, the more it's there. The bigger it grows."

"The more you do it, the more the anticipation fades, the more used to it you get, the less you obsess about it…"

"You're obsessing about it?" No, no, no. She wasn't going to start diagnosing him.

"I'm turned on by you all the time. All I have to do is think about your pajama pants and I get hard. But, for a guy, in lust, that's perfectly normal."

Drawing her legs beneath the chair as far as her knees would allow them to go, she said, "My pajama pants?"

He tried for a nonchalant shrug. Wasn't sure he pulled it off, so he went on the offensive—always a better way to be. "You going to tell me that you aren't still way too sexually aware of me since that night?"

She could try. Her lips had already given her away.

Jumping up, Meg crossed the room, rounded the corner where he couldn't see her. A few seconds later she came back, sans pajama pants. Because he was him, and she was her, and he liked to tease her, he considered telling her that the whole double shirt thing kept drawing his attention to her breasts, but wasn't sure he was up for a single shirt braless her that would show him the exact shape of nipples he could remember suckling...

Not until he could get his lips on them again.

His painful erection purposefully hidden by the table, he waited for her to give them the go-ahead. He was going to take it slow, lights on, wanting to know, explore and pleasure every single part of her. But it would happen in her time, not his.

That night or a different one.

When she sat back down, meeting his gaze, not, then meeting it again, he was ready to give her anything she asked.

"You're gorgeous, Danny." Words that should have pleased him. Her practical tone of voice, the way she shook her head, took away any pleasure he might have taken. "Of course, now that I've *seen* you in that way..."

"Experienced, you mean..."

"Okay, yes, experienced. Now that I've experienced you in that way, of course I'm aware of your... gifts...in the sexual arena."

Sex with a therapist. Her approach should have dampened his desire. It had the opposite effect.

"Of course, I feel...attraction, probably more so since I'm in the beginning stages of bringing your child to life..."

His zipper dug into tender skin.

"And if I was different, I'd be willing to try your little...experiment. To test your theory. But... I'm not you, Danny. And in this area, I've never been like you, which is why we never explored a physical relationship between us in the past."

"And here I thought it was because I didn't turn you on."

"I didn't turn you on, either."

"I never let myself think of you that way. Other things were more important."

"Exactly."

"But we've done it, Meg. We've crossed over. We need to let it play out, to burn itself out, so we can get back to who we were. Even if we didn't have a coming child to raise... I miss you. I need your friendship."

Her smile comforted, even as it warned.

"And I need your friendship, too," she said softly, her eyes unusually moist.

Was she going to cry?

"And that's why I can't test your hypothesis," she said then, the strength in her voice returning. "I don't know how to have sex without emotional commitment," she told him. "To me, the sex is like dessert after the meal. It's wonderful and decadent, but I have to eat healthy food before I can have it."

A comment about eating dessert off her body almost slipped off his tongue. He got it back at the last moment. But couldn't stop thoughts of licking fudge and whipped cream off her skin from traveling through his mind.

"When I give my body, I give my heart," she continued, and for the first time since he'd entered the room, his penis started to shrink. "Sex isn't just physical pleasure. It's the one tangible thing I give to my partner that no one else gets from me."

The words stunned him. All their years together and he'd never heard them. He knew how she'd raise her child, but didn't know much about her views on sex.

"If I climb into bed with you, I'm going to need more than you can give, Danny. And that, my friend, is what will mess us up permanently."

He wanted to fight back. Looked for the best argument. Drew a blank.

"Now this is irony for you," he quipped, finally. "The guy who's great at sex being told that he doesn't have what it takes to please the one woman he most wants in bed with him."

"I'm more apt to call it a cruel twist of fate," she said, meeting his gaze head-on.

"I can go with that, too."

"I can't lose you, Danny."

"Ditto." He should go, wasn't ready to spend the rest of the night alone in his room. "So…no more cold shoulder, okay? No matter what it is, we talk about it."

"Deal."

"You feel like some ice cream? I noticed a place just down the street…"

Her smile was the Madonna and his best friend all rolled into one. The epitome of untouchable woman, and right there giving him her heart. And her gratitude. "I'd love some ice cream."

They stood up. She grabbed her satchel.

"Might want to do something about the double shirt, braless look," he said, not quite yet able to tamp down the desire that flooded him at the sight of her.

And, in spite of knowing she was right about everything, he was flooded with regret when she hid herself from him to change clothes.

As soon as she dropped Danny off at the airport the next morning, Megan made an appointment to see her OB/GYN in California. They didn't need to see her until her eighth week, which she'd known, but she wanted the appointment on the books.

And texted the time and date to Danny as soon as she hung up.

She thought about him all the way to Blaine. Considered his theory that if they had sex, the desire would pall. Tried it on to see if there was any way she could fit into it.

Admitted how badly she wanted to join him in bed.

But knew that she couldn't.

Darkness engulfed her as she thought about their future. Pushing it aside, she told herself that she just couldn't picture the new them, yet, but that they'd get there.

Just like she couldn't picture herself as a mother, yet. Didn't mean she couldn't be a great one.

Samantha was waiting for her at the library—already at their table in the conference room. She'd given the teenager an empty journal the first time they'd met, but hadn't seen it since, until right then. Samantha was writing in it, and Megan stood outside the opened door for a few seconds, watching the minor miracle, not wanting to interrupt whatever thought Samantha was privately exploring.

When she saw the pen pause, she continued to the room, closing the door behind her.

Samantha was closed off at first. Arms crossed. Giving one-word answers. Megan couldn't just sit back and be patient. In a matter of days, a young man was going to have a permanent injunction notice on his record. If he was deserving, she wanted it to happen. For Samantha's sake, more than anything.

But if he wasn't...

And Samantha was losing the boy she loved, losing the support of her baby's father with so much frightening, and physical, change ahead of her...

So, she kept pushing. One question after another. From "how did you sleep," To "have you spoken with your parents today?"

They'd talked innumerable times over the past weeks about how much her parents loved her—sometimes eliciting happy memories from Samantha—but when she gave the teenager the reminder that morning, Samantha sat up, stiff as a board.

"Stop it," she said, her teeth gritted.

"Stop what?"

"Stop trying to build this beautiful little picture of me and my mom and dad, like we're this happy unit, forever and ever. World without end. Goodbye."

Every instinct in Megan's body went on high alert. As focused as she'd ever been, she sat completely still, schooling her features to remain calm, and asked, "I'm sorry, Sammie, the way you've talked in previous sessions...you have such happy memories." Was the real young woman fighting her way out of the brainwashing? With Carter out of the picture, was she finding the strength to break free?

That had been the hope.

Making Danny and the Eversons right, and she'd

celebrate their victory with an open heart. She genuinely wanted what was best for Samantha. Just as she would for her own child.

"Yeah, well, I didn't know things, then," Samantha said, her chin dropping to her chest.

"Know what things?" Were there ghosts in the Eversons' closets after all?

"Whatever," Samantha said, and then, with an unladylike snort, pushed the still open journal over to Megan.

I bleed.
He bleeds.
My tears are wiped with gentle cotton while I
am rocked and fed.
His are left to dry in salty streaks while he
works to feed himself.
I used to lie on soft whispery clouds of ignorance.
Now I just lie.

Megan read it three times. Slowly. And then asked, "Who are you lying to?"

The teenager shrugged.

"Can I look at some of the other pages?"

"Whatever."

The journal was more than half filled with poetic outpourings. Megan absorbed as much as she could, wanting to immerse herself in them, but couldn't turn Samantha's outlet into a piece of evidence, or a medical report.

She pushed it back in front of Samantha, folded her hands on the table, and said, "Tell me what you're lying about, Sammie."

The girl shrugged. And Megan came back with, "Who are you lying to?"

"I don't know, okay?" The girl sent a glare her way as she clipped out the words. And then she started to cry. Sobs so fierce, so overpowering, they had to hurt. Megan maintained her professional position for all of a minute and then crossed to the other side of the table, wrapping her arms around the young pregnant woman, and held on.

Chapter Seventeen

Danny was sitting in a hotel pub in Kansas that night, eating a solitary dinner at a high top in the corner, case files open to the side of his half-eaten pepper steak, when Megan called.

"I got your text," she said. "The Mallory case again?" A brother and sister fighting over an elderly parent. She wanted to keep the father at home with a full-time caregiver. He wanted the man sent to a care facility that would be about half the cost, thus preserving inheritance money. Sierra's Web—Danny—had been hired by the sister. A psychiatrist who specialized with elder care and mental function on Kelly's team had testified, and they'd won the case. The brother had just filed an appeal.

"Yeah. But I'll get our response written up tonight and file it in the morning. This one's pretty straightforward." He didn't jinx himself with counting wins before they happened, but a junior attorney on his first case could put the reasons for appeal to bed without research.

It was good to hear her voice. Probably too good, so he didn't mention the fact to her. He'd told himself he absolutely would not be calling her that night. Was glad that she'd just prevented him from making a liar out of himself.

And was busy wondering...had she had a change of heart? After a day to think about it, did she see the sense in his plan to move them through sexual territory so that they could reach the other side and get back to being them?

"I had a major breakthrough with Samantha today." Her words, the passion in her voice, threw his attention on a completely different avenue.

"You did?" he asked, feeling enthusiasm light a fire in him as well. Finally. He'd known Meg could do it. Just hadn't known if they'd have the time... "Is it Carter? Do we have more evidence for the restraining order? Not that we need it, but if Samantha can see the rightness of it, she's on the way to a healthy life."

They'd have possibly saved a life.

Or two, considering that an unborn child was also involved.

"I'm not certain it's Carter's fault, Danny. Or Bella's, either. Not consciously on their parts. I can't say any more right now. I've told Joe and Lindy that I prefer not to talk to them about today's session yet, and they've granted their daughter the privacy on the matter that she requested from me this morning. I just...wanted you to know."

He had to argue the restraining order case before a judge. He needed to know.

And he trusted her.

Winning an argument didn't matter if the person he was fighting for wasn't helped by the win. That was one fact he never lost sight of.

A promise he'd made to himself when he passed the bar.

One he'd made to Megan along the way, too.

"I'm actually not sure anyone's at fault..."

They'd had other cases where she couldn't tell him everything she knew as soon as she knew it. It was part of the job. He'd never taken the lack of sharing personally before.

"She hasn't told me much. She was exhausted. We're meeting again in the morning."

He'd witnessed Megan at work during a break-through event. Had seen the overwhelming amount of emotion that such occurrences generated in the patient.

And she hadn't had to call. Didn't owe him the heads-up.

"Thanks for letting me know."

"I told Lindy and Joe I would. They were focused on Samantha."

"So, the three of them are talking?"

"I can't answer that. If Samantha wants to, they will. I'm not sure she'll even try. Not tonight, anyway. They know not to push."

Why couldn't he allow the not knowing? Why in the hell was it bothering him so much? It was nothing new. And yet…with Meg, it felt new.

It felt like a threat.

To whom they were.

"I have one more question, understanding that if you can't answer, you won't. Do you feel that someone not on our radar has hurt her in some way?" Did they need to get the police involved?

"No. And I assured the Eversons of that as well."

Then it was out of his hands for the moment. "Okay, well, thanks for the call…"

"You got a minute?"

A nonprofessional minute, he translated.

"Of course, what's up?"

She'd given his theory some thought? Was willing to consider that maybe if they just slept together a few times…

"I had some clarity today, listening to Samantha, talking to her. I found that I also needed to hear what she needed me to say."

Pushing his plate away, Danny closed the case file. "I'm listening."

"You can't always have what you want. Life doesn't work that way."

So he wasn't getting the sex he thought would solve everything. "Makes sense."

"It's not that you have to settle, but sometimes life has something better in store ahead, but you have to go through something first to be ready for it when you get there."

It wasn't typical Meg speak, and Danny wasn't sure what to make of it. Or her.

"Sometimes you find your happiness by making the best of what's in front of you."

That would work…if they were strangers giving truisms. Not sure how it applied, specifically, or why she'd felt it important to call him with it.

Unless…she was telling him to be satisfied with what they had and not push the sex. He'd broken one of their core rules in her hotel room the night before.

What an ass.

She didn't feel safe around him. Because he'd kissed her without warning or permission…

"Meg, I—"

"We have to face it, Danny," she interrupted him. "The friendship we had…it's done. We both want it, but we screwed it up and just because we want it doesn't mean we can get it back. It's like you said last night, and proved so conclusively, I might add…the sexual element is here now. There's no going back. And we've both always known that sex is the one place where we can't meet. It's why we stayed away from it for so long."

He'd heard somewhere that words could be like arrows. Hers were sharp, with meticulous aim, piercing him in the heart.

"I don't know where my life is going to lead me," she continued, "but I know I have to be honest. With you and with myself. I'm not going to have what I've always thought I wanted. Marriage first and then children with the love of my life. I might find the love of my life, waiting somewhere in my future. Maybe this experience will prepare me for him or lead me to him, but for now, I'm going to embrace being a single mom…"

She took a breath, leaving room for him to speak.

His throat was too constricted.

"I'm going to find my happiness here."

He was genuinely glad to hear the last words. Proud of her. She'd had a lot of time alone over the past weeks, time trapped in a hotel room far from anyone she knew, other than the job. While he'd been busy flying all over the States, taking on different challenges, filling his mind with law and legal issues.

And thoughts of sex with her, interspersed with the knowledge—slowly sinking in—that in a matter of months, he was going to be a father.

He'd taken out the new life insurance policy.

And made a plan, as yet unacted upon, to move to California.

She'd gotten her whole life under control. So Meg, to get there way ahead of him.

"Where do I fit in?" So him, to run to her with his questions.

At twenty, that had been fine. Not anymore. He was an adult, needed to find his own solutions.

"You're the father of my child."

Practically speaking, the answer was clear as mud. Relief flooded him anyway. At least she wasn't going to try to take that away from him.

"We'll be raising the child together. Co-parenting."

"Unless you tell me differently." More relief. So much he felt weak there for a second.

"But, Danny, I need you to understand," she continued. "Our telling each other everything, relying on each other, holding each other sacred… I can't do it anymore. I'm going to end up jealous, wondering who you're with, hurting for no good or fair reason, wanting what I can't have, which leads to resentment…and that is absolutely not how I'm going to raise my child. Or treat an old friend."

And, boom.

He understood.

He told her so. Told her to keep him posted regarding the Everson case. Hung up.

And ordered a beer.

* * *

Megan didn't regret her conversation with Danny. Didn't regret the decisions she'd made. She knew they were right for her. The healthiest choice.

Better for her heart to shatter, and have time to heal, before the baby arrived, rather than afterward.

Knowing that she'd lost Danny's friendship wasn't even much of a shock. The idea had been growing on her for weeks. Since the predawn moment she'd woken up naked in his bed.

She worried about him, though. Danny didn't have a lot of close friends. He had a slew of casual people in his life.

She could cry her eyes out. And did, the night she'd ended their friendship, and the next night, too.

Danny wasn't a crier. Had no good way to release a dozen years' worth of friendship.

He was no longer her best friend, but he was the father of her child.

The night after their breakup, she got up out of bed, dried her eyes and sat in the chair, right where he'd sat, looking out the window, as she texted him.

We will always be connected, through our child. We'll always be seeing each other, because of the baby we made. In a way, we're closer now, more connected, than we ever were. Just connected differently. And when all is said and done, maybe being part of a peripheral family will be better than being road buddies...

She had to stop typing when tears flooded her

eyes so badly she couldn't see the keyboard on the screen.

There was more.

And…what was she doing? Letting him go and dragging him back the very next night? Leaving her phone on the table, she crawled back into bed.

Without hitting send.

She didn't hit it the next morning, either, when she got up and saw her phone sitting on the edge of the table. She deleted the message instead.

In spite of the state of her personal life, or maybe because of it, Megan's work with Samantha was completely on task. She spent several hours with the young woman over the next few days, intense sessions unlike anything she'd ever done in her career, traveling through the murky tangle inside a very bright and caring young woman.

Samantha had real passion when it came to social consciousness. Hated social class. But had no answers for how to solve the problems that bothered her. Drug addiction. Homelessness. People who had so little when others had so much. Megan was left with the sense that Samantha had taken on the problems of an entire globe, problems that world leaders struggled with every day, that they'd been dealing with for centuries, and still hadn't solved. And yet, Samantha seemed to dislike herself for not having solved them.

The second full day, since she'd talked to Danny,

Megan asked Samantha to take a moment to think about what a perfect world for her would look like. And then asked her to describe the world.

She and Carter were married before their baby was born. They were living with Bella. They had a little girl, named Linda, they were both working hard, making enough money to help out with Bella's expenses, and both enrolled in online college courses, too. Other than the baby's name being a version of her mother's, which Megan considered critical information, Samantha made no mention of Lindy and Joe Everson, or of any part of her life on the ranch.

Nor had she seemed to have any vision beyond the next year or so.

When Megan mentioned adding the baby's maternal grandparents to the picture, Samantha adamantly shook her head and said, "That's not me."

She had a lost look about her after that, but Megan couldn't pull any more from her and chose to end the session.

They were making good progress, but helping Samantha unravel her thoughts and untangle her emotions was a precarious give and take. Give her time. Take what she could give in the moment.

The fact that the clock was running against them was robbing them of the "time" portion of the dance.

Giving herself time was why Megan almost didn't answer as the car's hands-free audio system announced an incoming call from Danny that afternoon. After her session with Samantha, she'd decided to take a drive along Wisconsin's country roads rather than heading straight back to the hotel. She'd been seeking space apart from life to clear her mind.

To exist in a land where seemingly nothing existed.

But Danny was a partner on a case, albeit one who had become more adversary to her task than helpmate. She had to take his call.

"I have nothing to report as of yet," she said immediately after the "Hey, Danny" that came out sounding unbelievably fake. And then, before he could so much as a get a "hey" back, she continued. "Her life appears to be consumed by Carter, to the point of shunning any part of herself that attaches to her parents, as it would be if she was being brainwashed or manipulated. But she exhibits no intimidation, fear, or even discomfort at the mention of her boyfriend, which I would expect to see in the case of manipulation."

"Good to know." Danny's voice, deep and familiar, spread through her, warming her. Until she quickly shut off the faucet. Time. She needed time. "But I'm not calling about the case."

Then what? She didn't want to ask. Didn't want problems in her current space, out in the middle of nowhere where she could just rest and not seek answers.

So that, when she was ready, she'd be able to find and implement the best solutions. Even when they were hard. Or hurt.

Giving birth hurt. But women did it every day and a new life was born. Often with rejoicing. Bringing more love into the world.

She had to hurt to find her new life. Didn't make the finding wrong.

"I don't give up easily, Meg."

Of course, he didn't. A trait that made him an expert lawyer.

"I fight for what I believe in."

Why did he feel the need to tell her things she already knew?

But she knew why.

She just...couldn't...

"Fair warning," he said, and then hung up.

She didn't call him back.

Chapter Eighteen

Danny flew from Kansas to California and was following a realtor from one home to another when Megan called the next day. Originally, he'd thought that she might go with him to look at places. Ironic that she'd called at that exact time, not in the evening, as usual.

With a button on his steering wheel, he answered on the first ring. "Hey, there!" He didn't even attempt to keep the pleasure out of his tone.

"This is about the case, Danny," she answered. "I just left Samantha, and I'm calling as an expert therapist for Sierra's Web working with you on this case to request that you consider speaking with your client about canceling the request for a restraining order."

"Even if I wanted to, we can't cancel it at this

point. For the sake of the victim. Abusers get to their victims, intimidate them, or use love against them, to get them to back down. That's just standard. The judge has to hear the case."

"You can make a motion to the judge, with my expert testimony stating that it's in the victim's best interest to deny the request, so he can consider denying the order without anyone having to go to court. There's a good chance he would do so, since, in this case, it's the victim's parents, not the victim asking for the cancellation to begin with. Not likely the alleged abuser would be able to turn them. And while you could make the argument that their daughter could have turned them, that she got to them, begging them to trust her and not do this, but no one's going to get to me."

According to GPS, he had fifteen more miles to travel on Highway One before his turnoff. "Are you sure about that?"

"What does that mean? You're doubting my professional ability now?"

Whew. She was maaaddd. "Samantha Everson does seem to be affecting you more than other cases we've worked on together."

"I am perfectly capable of doing my job, Daniel Tremaine. And doing it well. I told you from the beginning that I didn't think a restraining order was the right approach."

Before she knew she was pregnant.

Like Samantha.

But she had a point.

And his job was to listen to it. And then determine whether or not he had reason to question her judgment.

A harsh thought. One he didn't like having.

And wasn't sure was biased, either. Megan had given him no cause whatsoever to doubt her professionalism. Or her ability.

"I apologize," he said with a weary sigh. "Please continue."

"Samantha is definitely struggling with mind games, but I'm not sure Carter's the one playing them on her..."

"Surely you don't think Joe or Lindy..."

"Would you please let me finish before you jump in with your argument?"

"Sorry. Yes."

"And maybe try to listen with an open mind, rather than with an ear to what argument you can use against me?"

Touché. "Again, I apologize."

"I think the culprit might be Samantha herself," she told him, and, blinking, he sat up straighter.

So like his Meg to throw a wrench he had hadn't even contemplated. "I don't follow," he told her, but his brain was working on it. "She's manipulating herself?"

"Yeah, sort of. Not purposefully, or even consciously, but I'd bet my career on it."

He'd never heard that one before.

But then, he'd never heard she was giving up on their friendship before, either.

Stop.

They were working.

She'd asked for his professional attention and she was going to get it.

"I'll need something more concrete than that to go to the Eversons." And he didn't hold any hope at all that Joe and Lindy were going to change their minds. He'd spoken with them that morning.

"I don't have enough, or Samantha's permission, to give it to you, yet. But I can tell you how I base my theory. Being with Carter and Bella has put Samantha in a battle of haves and have-nots, most definitely, but I think the battle comes more from her own culture shock than it does anything Carter or Bella has done or said. Carter maybe exacerbates it by needing her, and her not really fitting in his world, so she's adamant about fitting in because she needs him, too. They're young adults in love. Dealing with turbulent, hormonal emotions and impending parenthood as well.

"But that's not all of it. She's fighting her parents' supposed image of her, too, and though I don't know this yet, I have a feeling she's decided she doesn't measure up. I believe it's probable that she feels like a huge disappointment to them…"

"There's no way—"

"I'm not saying she is a disappointment to them, or that they're in any way responsible for making her feel like she's not good enough for them, or in any way a disappointment. I'm saying that Samantha spends a lot more time analyzing society and life, caring about the problems of others, than a lot of kids her age. She's more aware of the needs and feelings around her at a time when most kids her age tend to be more self-absorbed. And, being that she and Joe and Lindy were a team for her entire life, she probably feels as though she knows them as well as she knows herself. She feels she knows what they do and don't like, what they do and don't want, what they do and don't hope for—and I suspect that in her estimation, all of their likes and wants and hopes for her have been dashed…"

Rounding a precarious curve, Danny caught a great glimpse of the ocean running alongside him—mostly dozens of feet below the cliffs he was traversing—and reminded himself that he wasn't going to let Meg dash his hopes. But shook his head and tuned back in immediately, finding her conversation engrossing.

"She hasn't said as much yet, that she feels like she's disappointed her parents, but if I had to make a diagnosis right now, based on everything she's said, her mannerisms at key moments, what she's guarding and not saying, what I've observed from everyone since I've been here, this is it. She's manipulating, or brainwashing, herself.

"Certainly, the diagnosis explains why she'd be resentful of them, and resistant to being at the home she grew up in. At the moment they're all reminders of her failures. Reminders that she no longer belongs. And reminders of the love she feels she's losing there. That she has to lose because she can't be who they expect or need her to be. Again, this would just be in her mixed-up thinking. I am not saying that Joe and Lindy Everson have in any way indicated any of this to Samantha, feel it, or would ever love her less."

The theory made one hell of a lot of sense. Puzzle pieces all fit into place. And yet... Joe and Lindy were convinced that it was Bella and Carter who had transformed Samantha.

"How do you suggest we proceed?" he asked, reminding himself that he'd listen before arguing. Listen for the possibility of new solutions, not just to argue.

"We just need more time, Danny. The minute that injunction order is permanent, we risk losing her. Period. If I can't help her find a balance within herself, help her through her inner struggles, before the court date, we could be signing her death warrant. Or to be less dramatic, her desire to run away warrant."

She wanted him to cancel the order. Period. He'd

been hoping for something more…to give to Joe and Lindy.

"Have you suggested that Samantha talk to her parents?" he asked. "If she could tell them how she feels about being at home, what about it makes her unhappy or uncomfortable, if she could try and explain why she feels like she doesn't fit in…"

"A dozen times, at least," Megan said. "That's why I need more time. She's not to the point of articulating, even to herself, the things I explained here. She won't talk to them."

"Which leaves them completely frustrated and feeling as though they have no option but to proceed. For the record, they say that Samantha has been better these past few days, more like her old self in terms of the way she speaks to them—not the words, but the tone she's using. Caring. Loving. They said she hasn't been this way since the first weeks she started dating Carter." He gave her the last statement very succinctly. "They're certain it's because he's been out of her life and hasn't been able to be in contact, to manipulate her."

"When, in fact, it could be that she's desperate to get him back and is pulling out all the stops with me in an attempt to do that."

"She needs to talk to them, Meg. I think she'd be the only one to help them see."

"I said pretty much the same thing to her this afternoon. She won't do it."

Frustration rose up within him. The car that had just darted in between him and the realtor he was following, and then slowed down, didn't help matters.

"Kind of like you won't talk to me," he said, and bit his bottom lip as soon as the words escaped. They weren't fair.

He wasn't taking them back.

"Maybe she has tried, like she says, Danny. Maybe they won't listen like you aren't listening to me."

He didn't even try to hold his tongue, then. "I am listening, Meg. About Samantha, and us, too. I'm even hearing. I just have a different perspective regarding us than you, as do the Eversons regarding their daughter. Now, I can't speak for the Eversons. I'll relay to them what you said, but my professional opinion is that they aren't going to cancel the order. I'm not even sure they could bring themselves to try at this point."

"What are you going to recommend to them?"

"I see merit in what you're saying. If it were up to me, I'd give you the time. And I'll tell them that. But if they want to proceed, I'm going to do so. It's my job, to give them their choices, in terms of legalities, and then to do their bidding. And I also believe that's the right thing to do. She's their daughter. As long as they have Samantha's best interests at heart, and are listening to expert opinions, seriously considering them, then they should have the last word."

"I respect that."

He heard her voice come over the car speaker, but had to sit there for a second, hardly daring to believe he'd heard what he thought he had.

At the same time, realizing the ridiculousness of his reaction. Meg always listened to understand. Not to fight. Or win. To understand.

The reminder was one he'd needed. Valuable.

"And about us, Danny? Are you really hearing what I'm saying?"

"Loud and clear." He took a deep breath, and dove in. "I just don't agree, Doc."

"Danny…" Tension was back in her voice.

"Hold on," he said. "I listened and now I have right to speak."

"Point taken."

"I'm not going to be like some kind of creep who stalks you. Nor even an irritant who won't leave you alone. Sex is completely off the table. I get that. Agree with it. But the rest…you're my best friend, Meg, whether I'm yours anymore or not. You're in my heart, and I'm holding you there."

"Danny, I can't…"

"I'm not asking you to. I'm telling you I am. I'm coming to you, being honest with you, because that's who you are to me. What you do is what you do."

"But…"

"I'm not putting any expectations on you, Meg. I

accept whatever you can or can't give me. Those are your choices to make. This is mine."

"I just…"

He waited for her to finish. When she didn't, he said, "It's a heart thing, not a mind thing, Doc."

He'd never seen himself as a heart thing kind of guy. But then, he'd never faced losing Megan. And if Samantha could have hidden sides to herself, well, then, he could, too.

"I'll call you tomorrow, after I speak with the Eversons," he said.

"Okay. Thank you."

His thumb was on the button to disconnect the call when she said, "Where are you?"

He'd said he was going to be honest with her. Didn't want to raise any more tension between them. "Why?"

"No reason. None of my business, actually. You just didn't say, and I realized I didn't know if you're still in Kansas or on another job. Forget I asked. I'll wait to hear from you in the morning."

She clicked off, and as he drove down the highway, he was smiling.

Meg still cared.

There was no place she could go to escape Danny. If she walked, he was there, reminding her of their awkward Riverwalk night. The other way down the street was the ice cream shop.

In the hotel…he was everywhere.

She'd driven until she was tired of driving.

And in her room…she could hardly get naked long enough to shower without wanting Danny.

But she knew where it would lead. She knew her. And knew him, too.

It wasn't like Samantha Everson at all. The teenager was confused, unsure of who she was. She and Danny were adults, and they'd talked often about what they wanted out of life. And what they didn't want.

What they were good at.

And where they failed.

He wasn't a settling down kind of guy. The very idea of it stripped him of his Danny-ness. Made him tense, just to talk about it. Always had.

And she was…a woman who wanted a home and family. And one who knew him well enough to know that he'd feel trapped by the very things she needed most.

Which would trigger her trust issues.

It was a recipe for disaster and there was no way, in good conscience, she could let it happen.

Yeah, she loved the travel that was part of their jobs, but she didn't get high on it like Danny did. She got high on helping people. And on meeting up with Danny in all of their various cities all over the country. She got high on exploring those cities with him.

Eating out together and staying in rooms with adjoining doors.

But that part of her life was done.

In her new chapter, she was going to love his baby, instead.

She'd just finished dressing in the newly dry-cleaned blue suit she was donning for the third time since she'd arrived in Milwaukee, and was heading to the door to leave her room the next morning when Danny called to tell her that the Eversons were not going to cancel their motion for a permanent injunction order. The hearing would go on as planned the following day.

He'd prepared her, but she was still deeply disappointed.

"I'm assuming they aren't going to want my testimony," she said then, trying not to think about the fact that Danny would be back that night. In the adjoining room. She'd already had notification from Sierra's Web that his reservation was confirmed—the usual course of events when they were on a job together and rooming side by side.

"I advised them that it would best not to call you to the stand," he admitted, as though he'd done something wrong, but she'd known that part would be a given. Would have disrespected him if he hadn't done so. "However, they insist that they still want you to give your expert opinion to the judge."

Well, that made no sense at all. "It's going to hurt their case."

"As I also pointed out, at which time they reminded me that it's not about winning or losing a case, it's about doing all they can to see to their daughter's best interests. They recognize that, as deeply involved as they are, they aren't able to be impartial…"

"Wow."

"Yeah. Kind of makes you wonder about us, doesn't it? With everything that's happened in such a short amount of time, how can we possibly look at our situation impartially?"

"Would you quit comparing us to this case? Please?"

"It's not just this case, Meg. It's life. You learn about life, about what you want and don't want, about what seems right for you, to you, and what doesn't, by what you see and experience as you live your life. You're the one who taught me that, and you're right. And when you consider all of the different people we see, all across the country, from all different walks of life…we can't help but be shaped by them. Learn from them."

He was right, of course. "So, the difference between the Everson case, and us, is that we aren't being manipulated, Danny. We know our own minds. We're comfortable in our own skins, not acting out of character, lashing out, or turning on those we love."

"You're kind of turning on me. Cutting me out of your friendship sphere."

She'd hurt him.

She couldn't believe how much, actually. Hadn't thought he'd take her decision so hard. Had kind of thought he'd welcome it, as it let him off the hook of any unwanted expectations she might build.

With her satchel still on her shoulder, she sank down on the end of the unmade, and far too tousled bed where she'd just spent another hellish night. "I'm not cutting you out, Danny."

"Your words, Meg. We aren't us anymore."

"No, but you're going to be a major part of my life. Just…differently." The text she'd composed the other night and then hadn't sent…she should have. "I need the ground rules I set. My heart needs time to get to know the new us, but at no point did I even consider no us."

"You're confusing me, Doc."

"I know. Probably because I'm confused myself, but think about it, Danny. We'll always be together in some form because of the baby we made. Who we are, how we've agreed we want to raise our child, kind of made that a given. In a way, we're closer now, more connected, than we ever were. Just connected differently. And when all is said and done, maybe being part of a peripheral family will be better than being road buddies." She hadn't sent the text, but she'd saved it in her mind. And thought of it multiple times, including the night before when she'd been lying in bed, missing him.

Hating that she didn't know where he was.

"I guess you'd want to know that I found a house just off Highway One, then."

Her satchel sat alone on the bed as she walked to the window, looked out, then paced to the door. "You're in California?"

She had to pee. Her heart was thumping. All the extra energy rushing through her. Anticipation. Fear. Happiness. Dread. Overwhelmed, she sat back down by her satchel.

"I'm meeting with the realtor this morning to make an offer. The place is special, Meg, one of a kind, giving me a bit of Colorado and a whole lot of California all in one. Up on a cliff, overlooking the ocean, but with an eight-foot wrought-iron fence around the entire property to keep little ones from running off to danger…"

He was buying a house within a few miles of her condo! What if he was acting too rashly? Would he regret the move? Start to feel trapped?

"Are you sure this is what you want to do? You've got lots of time."

"What I wanted to do was have you look at it. See what you think, but with the whole no friend thing…"

He was really buying a house! With or without her! The smile that broke out from deep within her spread to her face. Pulling her laptop out of her satchel, she sat at the table and opened up. "Send me the address. I can pull it up here and take a virtual tour."

He did so. And stayed on the phone with her as she looked at all of the specs, the photos, going through room to room with her. And then out to the huge, grassy backyard and in-ground pool and outdoor kitchen.

She loved the place.

Absolutely loved it.

For him and for their child, she carefully reminded herself.

What a wonderful place to spend time growing up.

And if he changed his mind later...she could always buy it from him.

By the time they hung up, he'd emailed his offer to the realtor.

The peripheral family part of their lives together had officially begun.

Chapter Nineteen

By 9:00 a.m. California time, Danny was already with his realtor, signing the acceptance of his offer, and making closing arrangements. Since he was paying cash for the house, he only needed time to move the money out of one of his investments, but the title company needed a little longer. The inspection would be happening later that day. The home he'd just purchased had been a vacation house for the couple he'd purchased it from, and they could be moved out by the following weekend.

Anticipation filled him, and when Sheila, the broker he'd been working with, asked to treat him to breakfast at a great place she knew near his new home, he gladly accepted. The avocado breakfast casserole, served with fresh fruit garnish, that she'd recommended had been delicious, as had been the smiles and conversation.

Sheila was gorgeous, interesting, had lived on the California coast her entire life and owned her own brokerage firm. She loved to surf and had offered to teach him. He was right there with her until she asked him if he'd like to have dinner the next time he was in town. And smiled in the way that added sex to the menu.

He gave her his regretful smile, truly did feel sorry that he had to disappoint or embarrass such a nice person, but couldn't accept her invitation.

Because he didn't want to have dinner with her. Or sex, either, oddly enough, considering how randy he'd been.

He'd just bought his first home. Meg loved it as much as he did. It was close to her. And she wasn't done having him in her life—just changing him from friend to peripheral family.

All before ten o'clock in the morning.

The excitement coursing through him was far better than dinner.

Or sex.

Samantha hadn't known that Megan was going to reach out to Danny to try to get the Eversons to drop the injunction order request, which, considering the outcome, was a good thing. The teenager, in jean shorts, a peasant top and brown sandals, her blond hair hanging long and straight, was agitated from the second she walked through the library.

Megan had arrived purposefully early, not wanting Samantha to have to wait alone for her to arrive, and she knew, just by the slump of Samantha's shoulders, and the sluggish gait of her walk that she wasn't in a good place. The sullen look on her face as she came in pretty much sealed the deal. Megan hadn't expected the pacing though. That was new.

"Have a seat, Sammie," she said softly after the girl had taken several turns around the end of the table.

As Samantha came closer, her belly at Megan's eye level across from her, she noticed that the young woman was starting to thicken around the waist.

And felt a sudden new kinship with her. It would be weeks yet before Megan started to show. Samantha was younger by far, a patient, and yet, ahead of Megan in one of life's most incredible, most memorable and lasting experiences.

She couldn't fail the pregnant teen. Period.

"You're clearly uptight, today, what's on your mind?" she asked, a bit blunter in her beginning of the session than normal. Whether Samantha's mind needed more time or not, they were out of it.

Samantha rolled her eyes.

"Tomorrow's the hearing," Megan continued, pulling more from her instincts than any set course of action she'd laid out for herself.

Everything depended on Samantha. Her mood. Her emotional accessibility.

The look in the young woman's pale blue eyes could have bored holes. Megan was impervious to it. She bored right back. "Time's up, Sammie. You need to talk to your parents. Really talk. Like you talk to me, only more."

She shook her head. "You just don't get it. Talking to Mom and Dad isn't going to change anything. I've tried. Like a gazillion times. They just don't get it."

"Get what?"

"That people change." An answer. Finally. An honest to God answer.

To some the response might just seem like three clichéd words. Innocuous. Megan's adrenaline was pouring through her.

"You've changed," Megan said.

Samantha nodded.

"Tell me how."

Her snort was not at all elegant. "Duh, I'm seventeen and pregnant," she said with a good bit of sarcasm.

"And you believe they think less of you because of that?" She walked an incredibly careful line between extracting what was there, and leading Samantha to think something was there that wasn't. The former she had to do quickly. And by doing so, risked doing the latter.

"Wouldn't you?" Samantha threw the question back at her.

"Absolutely not. I might be disappointed for my daughter's sake, because, having been through having and raising a child, I could see some hardships ahead that she might not yet see, and I might hurt for the struggles I know she'll be facing, but no way does my opinion of her, or my love for her change." The Eversons were having Megan testify in court, in spite of the fact that they knew she was against the restraining order. That told her all she needed to know about the couple. And so felt more comfortable presenting in court what she suspected would be close to what they could say for themselves, had their daughter given them an audience, as she had Megan.

"Yeah, well, you don't know what it's like, growing up out in the country, living on a big ranch, where pretty much everyone is treated like family and everyone knows everything about everyone."

"No, I don't. Why don't you tell me about it?"

Samantha spent the next twenty minutes talking about her life on the ranch, painting an emotional picture of a lovely childhood. One she'd determined she'd irrevocably ruined.

"But you know what sucks?" she asked suddenly.

"What?" Megan had no idea what was coming.

"They preach to me about being aware of others, their plights, about the importance of giving, not just receiving, helping not just having people do for you, and all the while they were letting me grow up in a make-believe world."

Leaning forward, Megan frowned. "How so?"

"I couldn't figure out why Carter wouldn't take me home," she said. "We dated for a whole month, he'd come to my house, but he'd never let us hang out at his place. He wouldn't introduce me to his mom. So, I went to the diner where he said she worked, just to introduce myself, you know. Because, I don't know why. I just did. And she was so wonderful and sweet. And super excited to finally meet me. She invited me over for dinner. And…wow. They live in two rooms, with a hole in the bathroom floor where you can see down to the ground beneath, but can't afford to have it fixed. Bella bought the place for a steal when Carter was little because she'd had problems with her landlord trying to make her do things just to get repairs done and stuff. Their table was clean, but all scratched up. The silverware was mostly castoffs from the diner, and one time I pricked myself on a bent tine and they both felt so horrible. Them? Seriously. I was the one who'd grown up unaware how hard life is for some people. I ate off real silver, and while I knew not everyone did that, and I knew that my dad worked really hard and made a lot of money, and was generous to his employees and others, I had no idea… I felt so guilty going home that night…"

Enthralled at the miracle happening, yet so pained

by the distress she was witnessing, Megan didn't interrupt. Or even move. Her job was to take it all in.

"And from then on, it just got worse. Then Carter and I, well, it just happened and, of course, one time and I end up pregnant. But, you know, the baby… it was like a cleansing. I wasn't that blessed girl on the ranch anymore. I could start out fresh. Part of the Wilson family. We had plans. Good ones. Smart ones. But no, my parents have to ruin it all. Because I'm not like they want me to be."

Taken with all Samantha had said in the past, Megan knew her diagnosis of the night before had been spot-on. Didn't matter a whit. Not if she couldn't work another miracle and help Samantha find more in herself before the next morning.

"When you were talking a little bit ago, about your life on the ranch, you sounded happy."

"I was! Who wouldn't be! But that wasn't real life."

"Actually, it was, Samantha. A very real life. Different from Carter and Bella's, yes. But equally valid. Just as there are people much more successful, living much more opulently, than your parents. Life is filled with atrocity, and with beauty. Some are born to one life, some to others. Like a little girl I saw not too long ago who'd been born to a drug addict. Why? How fair was that to that child? I don't have those answers. And the truth is, neither do you."

The girl stared at her wide-eyed as Megan continued. "What matters is that you're aware. That you want to help."

"I do want to help. Starting with raising my child to be aware that…"

"That what?"

The girl shrugged.

"You want to raise your child without anything so that…what? It's more aware of how it feels not to have? You think it's better to be raised with want, than not?"

"I don't know." Samantha's tone raised to almost a cry as she shook her head.

"Or were you afraid that if your parents saw Carter's house, they'd think less of him? Maybe not let you see him?"

"That's kind of what happened, isn't it?" the girl asked. "That injunction order is because they think he's after my money. But he's not. I haven't even told Carter, or his mother, about my trust fund. I was too ashamed."

It made her different from them.

"Let me ask you something else," Megan continued, sorting, learning…feeling. "Do you love your parents?"

No answer. And then, with tears starting to brim in her eyes, Samantha said, "Yes."

"So what happens to that part of you when you marry Carter and move in with Bella?"

Samantha shook her head.

"And what happens to their grandbaby who'll want to know them? And who they'd love as completely as they've always loved you?"

Tears dripped down Samantha's cheeks. "It's a cluster," the girl said. And then, pounding the palm of her hand on the edge of the table said, "There's no way out."

And there. They'd reached Samantha's core. One that felt trapped and hopeless. From there they could build a ladder and help her find her way out.

If they had more time.

"You've got tonight, Samantha," Megan said. "You said people change. You've changed. Have you given your parents a chance to see the change? Or are you too ashamed, too busy beating up on yourself, to take a chance that they'll still see you as the beautiful young spirit you are? And if they do, then how do you continue to shun them? Loving them and all?"

The girl met her gaze, not bothering to even try to hide the anguish pushing up from inside her.

"Carter's not going to like me going back to them."

Uh-oh. "Did he say so?" Was everything going to turn on a dime?

"No."

"Not ever?"

Frowning, Samantha shook her head, as though wondering why Megan was making such a big deal out of the question.

"No, he'd never criticize my parents! Carter's not like that," she said, and then continued, "But… I mean… I won't be like him anymore…so…"

"He liked you before you went to the diner and met his mom."

Samantha just sat. Megan guessed the girl's mind was spinning. Wished so badly she could reach in a finger and stop the blades before they bit into the girl even deeper.

"You've made a lot of determinations on your own, Sammie," she said quietly, instead. "You're a bright young woman, with a huge heart. And you want what's best, even to your own detriment. But you're taking on things that aren't yours to take on. And deciding for others what they feel or don't feel, think or don't think…"

Her words stopped her in her tracks.

Danny. Him believing they could still be best friends. Buying a house in California when she knew he was going to feel trapped eventually.

Not listening to what he said, but to what her mind told her she knew about him.

People changed.

She couldn't think any further about it at the moment.

But she knew she had to. The second she had personal time.

"So here's where I think we're at," she said then, a firmness to her voice that came of its own accord.

"You're making adult decisions. If you want the right to make more of them, then you need take accountability for one of the hardest things about being a healthy adult—honest communication. Be responsible to your thoughts, by sharing them fairly and accurately, and be willing to listen in the same way. Part of that is understanding that in healthy adult relationships, there isn't a boss and kid or a winner and loser. There are only equals who are different from each other, who have to work together to find something that works between them."

The girl met her gaze again. Held it. Nodded.

"What happens if you love someone who won't listen like that, or isn't willing to work together to find that something?"

"That's when you have to make smart decisions on your own. May I ask who, specifically, you're referring to?"

"My parents."

"And the injunction order?"

The girl nodded.

"You love them. You know they mean well. And you know they have not only the legal right, but the legal responsibility for the next several months, to make executive decisions on your behalf. To override you."

The girl nodded. Not happy. But no longer agitated. "Thank you."

Megan wanted to hug her. And couldn't. Not only

because of the table between them, but because she was a professional, doing a job.

Hoping that the pregnant teen got a huge hug in the immediate future from her loved ones, she stood and said, "You're right in that you've changed, Sammie. Welcome to adulthood."

Samantha smiled. Nodded, and reached out her hand.

Megan took it. Held on.

And then let go.

Chapter Twenty

With the three-hour time difference between LA and Milwaukee, Danny landed past dinnertime that night, but Meg was there to get him. She'd texted to tell him she'd pick him up from the airport.

They needed to talk, she'd said.

Words pretty well ominously accepted as a prelude to breaking up.

There was nothing to break up. As she so forcefully made clear—they weren't together and never would be.

He was looking forward to seeing her. And kind of dreading it, too, just until he got a clear understanding of what a peripheral family looked like.

She pulled up to the curb as soon as he exited baggage claim, timing her trip from the cell phone waiting lot perfectly, and as he dropped into the passenger seat, he almost leaned over and kissed her.

Something he had absolutely never done before.

Never even thought about doing. Time to scroll down the whole peripheral family thing.

As it turned out, she'd just wanted to talk to him about the case, since they were first on the judge's docket in the morning. Samantha had had a major breakthrough and Megan felt better about her patient, injunction order and all.

She didn't give him much more. He couldn't ask. But wanted to know. Because it was…her. He wanted to share the victory with her.

"And I just want to tell you…the whole not listening to you thing, Danny, I was doing you a disservice, and I'm sorry," she said as she pulled up to valet parking outside their hotel.

His car door opened beside him, a red-suited gentleman asked him how his evening was going, while another took his bag out of the back seat. Meg exchanged information with the guy, collected her ticket, slipped the guy a few bucks and joined him, entering the busy lobby and heading toward the elevator.

Had she timed her announcement so that he had no chance to respond?

Of course, they didn't have the elevator to themselves. Some function had obviously just let out, and laughter and conversation swarmed around them from fancy dressed men and women, most of them seemingly not even noticing the couple in business clothes squeezed into the back.

Danny stepped closer to Meg, slightly in front of her. People might not know it yet, but the woman was pregnant. He had a baby to protect.

And the second they stepped off on their floor, and Meg made a beeline for her door, he reached for her forearm, pulling her to a stop. "No, no, no, no, no..." he said, letting go of her arm to wag a finger at her.

"What?" The wide-eyed look didn't work on him. He knew damn well the intelligent, never silent mind buzzing behind it.

"Not listening how? What disservice?"

"You know, the whole friendship thing. And wondering if you were ready to buy a house. I've been perceiving you from my own perspective and not listening to yours, and I'm sorry, that's all."

"So...you're ready to talk about friendship, again?"

"Not tonight...but I'm ready to listen. And to be open to mutual solutions," she said. "I can't agree to your casual sex caveat, but..."

"Stop with sex, Meg. It's off the table, okay? I was experiencing a major error in thinking there for a few, but the rest...we can talk about it?"

"Tomorrow, please? After the case?"

She looked beat. So much so that he wanted to

pick her up in his arms and carry her to bed, then lay beside her and listen to her breathe while she slept.

Not a friend thing. But not a sex thing, either. Maybe the peripheral family option? He didn't know, but figured she'd straighten him out. After the case was done.

He walked with her to her door, then moved to his, standing outside watching as she swiped her key card. "Night, Doc, sleep well," he said as the door clicked open.

"You, too, Danny. I'm glad you're here. I missed you."

With that, she was gone.

And he went in to take yet another cold shower.

In her black suit with a white-and-red blouse and red scarf, Megan hardly felt ready the next morning as she and Danny, also in a black suit with white shirt and black-and-white-striped tie, walked into the courthouse in Blaine, half an hour ahead of their scheduled hearing. His suggestion.

He wanted time with his clients, to go over what to expect once they entered the courtroom, and to answer any last-minute questions they might have.

It was when Danny was huddled with Lindy and Joe Everson, in a corner at the end of the hallway outside the courtrooms, that Samantha approached her.

"Is Carter going to be here?"

"I haven't heard specifically, but you can expect

him to be. He'll have an opportunity to present his case before the judge, to refute the arguments given for the permanent injunction order."

The girl, in green shorts with a short, but loose-fitting green-and-white top and white flip-flops, nodded. "I tried to talk to them last night. They wouldn't listen. Just like I told you."

She'd hoped. Hadn't known.

"They just kept saying that they felt strongly that Carter was the reason for the changes in my behavior, and that I needed time to figure things out."

"There's merit in that. You've done better this week, with the temporary restraining order in effect."

"They said all they want is my happiness."

"I fully believe that's true."

"Carter is my happiness. I've had a lot of time to think this week, but I've also cried a ton more. I might be getting my head together, but I'm definitely not happier and I just don't see why he has to be punished for my head trips."

Megan opened her mouth to spout some appropriate piece of advice, hadn't even been sure yet what, when Samantha cut her off. "But I have a plan. I'm doing what you said, being accountable for myself, and acting like an adult."

The words were ominous. Frightening, even.

At no point had Samantha exhibited any suicidal tendencies...but Megan had known the injunction order would push her to the limit.

"Samantha," she began, just as the little huddle at the end of the hall broke up. Samantha made a beeline for her parents.

To play the good little girl until after court and they got home?

She had to warn them.

"Danny," she said, going straight toward him. Needed him. "We've got to do something. Samantha's…"

Her words broke off as Carter and Bella entered the hallway from around the corner, accompanied by a professionally dressed—in brown tweed—fortyish looking woman, carrying a briefcase.

The unknown woman took stock of the people in the hall and made a quick beeline for Megan and Danny.

"I'm Cassie Hamilton, attorney for Carter and Bella Wilson. I need a minute with you, please," she said, leading Danny away.

And there Meg stood. Alone. Surrounded by hurting people. Hands tied. Her brain knew she'd done all she could, that she'd done her job and done it well. Her heart cried out, anyway.

She was watching Danny with Cassie Hamilton, relieved that the Wilsons had been able to afford an attorney, when Samantha approached, with her parents.

"I told them I have something to tell them, but I

want you here. I know you'll understand, but I'm not sure they will, and so maybe you can help?"

Exchanging a glance with the Eversons, receiving firm nods from both of them, Meg said, "Of course."

Standing so close to Meg, the pregnant teen's arm was touching hers, Samantha faced her parents. "First, I love you both…" She teared up, and then, taking a firm breath, stood straighter. "I know that you want what's best for me. And—" Samantha glanced at Megan "—Dr. Latimer has helped me see that I've been on kind of a collision course here and well, it's not Carter's fault. And it's definitely not Bella's. All she's done is try to be the best mom she can be to both of us. So, I promise to stay completely away from Carter, to have no contact with him or Bella whatsoever, until I turn eighteen, as long as you drop this whole injunction thing. It'll be on his record forever, Mom." Samantha held gazes with Lindy, who had tears dripping slowing down her face. "And on Bella's, too, and she doesn't deserve that. At all. Carter's the father of my baby, your grandbaby, and I love him." Samantha shrugged. "I can definitely do a year of hard time to make this all right for everyone."

Meg swallowed past a lump in her throat. Blinked.

And was saved from having to do anything but stand there fighting for composure as Joe and Lindy exchanged a glance, and Joe opened his mouth to speak.

Before he got words out, Danny approached. Megan had never been happier to see him, sought his gaze with her own, needing the silent communication that had always traveled so perfectly between them, needing his strength, but he went straight to Joe and Lindy. "Ms. Hamilton and Carter would like a word with you," he said.

Joe shook his head. "It's not necessary..." he started to say, but Carter darted forward, his attorney and mother coming after him, Bella, with a worried expression, reaching as though to pull him back.

"Please, Mr. Everson. All I wanted to tell you was that if you will please drop the injunction order against my mom, I'll stay away from Sammie until we're eighteen. I swear to God. I've already got plans to graduate high school in December, and then I've been accepted to a couple of colleges starting in January. I'm going to show you that I'll be a good provider, a good father, and if she'll still have me a year from now, a good husband to Sammie."

The young man never looked at his pregnant girlfriend. Maybe he couldn't and remain composed. Megan glanced at Bella, whose eyes were also moist, and then, like everyone else, looked at Lindy and Joe Everson.

"You gave the money to the owner of the diner to pay for my professional services on behalf of Carter and Bella, Mr. Everson," Cassie Hamilton spoke up beside Bella, and everyone in the huddle turned to face her. "Since I've done basically nothing here, let me earn my money by telling you that now would be a good time to speak to the judge before he gets peeved at us for holding up his court."

"You gave…" Samantha's jaw hung open as she stared at her father.

Megan had no idea what anyone else did in that moment, because Danny sidled up next to her, his hand in the small of her back, and said, "I think, other than my few minutes with the judge, our work is done here, Doc. Good job."

He was grinning his smart-ass grin, but the emotion in his eyes as they met hers, was confusing. Not Danny-like at all.

And not anything that she was going to be able to escape from.

No matter how loudly her brain was screaming at her to think smart and healthy.

Luckily Danny had work to occupy him in those moments after Carter and Samantha, each of their own accord with no communication between them, pleaded unselfishly, responsibly, for the motion for an injunction order to be dropped. Standing there, watching those kids…he'd been smacked so hard in the gut he hadn't been sure for a second there if he was going to recover.

Maybe he wouldn't. But he did his job. While Megan, bless Meg, did hers. As soon as Joe and

Lindy asked Danny to speak with the judge, and Cassie said she'd accompany him, Meg had rallied the five hurting people around her and had asked the questions that she always seemed to have at the ready to get them talking.

He didn't hear any of it, of course. He'd been taking care of business.

But in the car on the way back to Milwaukee, she filled him in.

There was still a lot of talking to do, but Carter and Bella and the Eversons were on the first step toward becoming a family. Carter would be graduating early as he'd planned and starting college. Samantha was taking some time to herself, and with her parents, to continue counseling with Meg, virtually, over the next few months. And Joe, Lindy and Bella all agreed to give permission for the young parents to get married before their baby was born, seven months along was the agreed upon time, and to work together to help raise the baby to a toddler while the child's parents got their educations.

An outcome he wouldn't have foreseen if he'd had years to work on the case.

Something he'd never have predicted.

And yet, it fit.

"Did you know before today that Joe gave money for Bella to hire an attorney?" Meg asked him as Milwaukee's high-rises came into view.

"I did. I suggested that he give it to the owner of

the diner so that Bella wouldn't know the source, and the attorney wasn't supposed to know, either. That was the whole point. So that no one could even have a thought to be prejudiced in Joe's favor because of the gesture. But he was so set at giving his daughter the best shot, and a little worried that he wasn't seeing things completely straight…but still had to go with his gut…that he wanted the other side fully and fairly represented. I have no idea how Cassie Hamilton found out about it."

"Bella said the owner of the diner told her. He thought she should know that she wasn't dealing with someone out to get her, but that Joe really was just looking out for the daughter he adored," Meg said. "Bella told Cassie, who apparently came today with both guns loaded, ready to prove that there was absolutely no cause to put any kind of injunction on either Bella or Carter. And to try to prove that Joe and Lindy Everson were wrong in their conclusions."

"You trying to tell me I might have lost my case, Doc?" He glanced over at her, afraid to linger more than a second even though he was stopped at a light, for fear of another slug of the intensity that had hit him in the courthouse hallway. "And that maybe I should have listened to you in the first place?" he added.

"I'm not always right, Danny."

Her tone…the way she was staring straight ahead…they weren't talking about the case anymore.

And he wasn't going to get into it with her while sitting behind the wheel of a car.

He didn't trust himself to keep the vehicle on the road.

Meg had expected Danny to have a flight booked out that afternoon. He didn't say anything about needing a ride to the airport. She'd originally planned to stay a few more days, at least, to be in Blaine for Samantha during the critical post injunction stage but would be booking a flight out the next morning.

Going home.

Danny wanted pizza from a vendor by the hotel—so like him to take them on a little exploratory side trip adventure—and she welcomed the suggestion.

Enjoyed just being with him for a moment, like old times.

Life was ahead. She'd deal with it. Find a way to be happy within it.

She was going to love being a mother. And knew that during the next days and weeks, she'd be consumed with thoughts of becoming one. Once she got home. And was living her own life.

Focusing on her own life.

They were back at the hotel by one with no plans ahead of them. At least she had none. Maybe one last trip to the Riverwalk. Maybe Danny would want to go with her. If he wasn't taking a cab to the airport. At any rate, she wanted to change out of work clothes.

Danny still hadn't mentioned his plans by the time they were upstairs. She went to her room. He went to his.

And maybe that was the new reality. Peripheral family. No longer best friends. Because if they spent too much personal time together, they'd end up in bed.

A phrase Samantha had uttered innumerable times over the past week came to mind. "Life sucks," she said aloud.

And Danny knocked. Had he heard her talking?

Pasting a smile on her face that she felt not at all, she pulled open the adjoining door.

He hadn't changed.

Neither had she.

He strode into the room. Owned it, as always. Stood at the window. Turned to face her.

And she paled.

Danny looked…sick. Or angry. Or…something.

Something was drastically wrong…

Open-mouthed, she approached him, but he held a hand up, staving her off. And everything inside her froze.

Danny had just rejected her.

Her heart barreled toward death.

She didn't know how she knew. Just did. Couldn't stop the freight train that was bearing down on her, ready to smash her into bits and pieces. Couldn't move, get off the tracks...

"I'm in love with you." His voice...so dry. And...

"What?"

"I'm in love with you."

She didn't get it. Any of it. "I love you, too, Danny." Was it about the friend thing? Had she really hurt him so badly? She hadn't even known she could, and if she'd known, she'd have died first.

He took a step forward, and then stopped. "No, Meg," he said, bending his head to peer directly into her eyes. "Listen to me. To my words. I. Am. In. Love. With. You."

He was...as in...man woman... She stared.

"I know," he said. "Go figure, right?" His grin attempt failed.

Only, it didn't really. The half grin, half pain-filled expression on his face jutted into her.

"I've been...for so long now... I couldn't figure it out. I'd be with another woman and want your laugh at what I said, not hers. Or she'd say something, and I'd rather hear what you'd have to say about it. I told myself...nothing, to be honest," he said. "I just went on. And then that night...when you kissed me... I didn't think. I just...did."

She was listening. Couldn't move. Not anything. Not her mouth. Her throat. Her gaze from his.

"Seeing Carter today, fighting for the woman he loved, or rather, being willing to sacrifice to do what he had to do to provide for his woman and child…it hit me. More like knocked me on my ass. I was jealous of him. I wanted to be him in our relationship. Not just a friend, or a peripheral family person… I wanted to be free to love you. Period. Whatever it takes."

She stared. Felt pressure behind her eyes. Couldn't swallow. Had to…needed to…should…

"You aren't saying anything."

"I…" She coughed instead of even getting the one syllable fully out.

"It's okay," he said then, nodding. "I know this is sudden, but I had to tell you. All these years…all of the superfluous relationships…it's because I was already taken. It's always been you. I just didn't want 'it' so I couldn't feel 'it' for you."

She opened her mouth again to speak. Couldn't leave him standing there, so vulnerable and open and…for her? But where words should have been there was a gulp of air.

And another. The pressure inside her exploded and she lurched forward, putting her arms around the only solid warmth she'd ever fully trusted, and started to sob. Hard wracking sobs that he absorbed without a word. He didn't rub her hair or her back. Didn't cajole or comfort.

He just held on.

For as long as it took.

She'd been running for so long.

From her own truth.

One too horrific for her to accept.

Because it had been the death of everything best in her life.

She couldn't be in love with Danny Tremaine. She couldn't be.

Or she'd lose him.

When her thoughts began to sharpen, she pulled back into herself, stepped away from him. Apologized.

And then stopped. Looked up at him, her chin trembling again. "I'm in love with you, too, Danny. More than anything. Which I'm sure is why I held back in every relationship." He'd joked about it weeks ago, but he'd been right. Poor Kurt. No matter how hard he'd tried, there was always Danny. And yet, she and Danny were just friends… best friends and no more for a very specific reason. Danny was Danny. Honest to the core, but kind of a womanizer. "I'm in love with you. I just—"

"Here's what I've figured out," he interrupted her. "Sex is like chocolate cake. Maybe you're a chocolate cake connoisseur. You're known for being an expert on chocolate cake. You travel the world overeating chocolate cake. Anywhere you go, you see a new chocolate cake recipe in a bakery window and it piques your interest. Until you have that one piece of chocolate cake that hits you so perfectly, the one that is made just for your taste buds, and nothing else measures up to it. You look at the other cakes and… they're just cake. They aren't ambrosia."

She was crying again. "So, what, Tremaine, you're telling me I'm a piece of chocolate cake?" she wailed through her tears.

"I'm telling you that while I appreciate good sex, no sex is good anymore if it isn't with you. And I'm telling you that even when we reach the stage of sex not being that new and exciting thing, being with you is the most exciting thing in my world, and I'm not going to do anything to lose that. To lose you. That's love Meg. And that's what you can trust."

"Danny…"

Trembling, she walked up to him, but didn't let herself touch him.

"What?"

"Would it bother you, greatly, if I asked you to marry me?"

"Are you asking?"

"Would it bother you if I was?"

"Are you?"

He was… Danny…not letting her be less than, give less than.

"I am."

"Then no, it wouldn't bother me."

What the hell!

"Daniel Lawrence Tremaine, will you marry me?" She was crying again. Smiling. Getting ready to lose herself in her man.

"Yes. And will you move into my new house with me and make it a home?"

"Yes."

"And if we have a boy, let me name him anything but Lawrence?" he asked.

"Yes. And will you please get those clothes off and let me climb on top of you?" She moved closer to him. Started in on the buttons of his shirt.

Their hands entangled on the second button. "Make up your mind, Doc. You want to do it, or you want me to? Because I can get it done a lot faster, and I'm not sure how long I'm going to last here."

She stepped back. Gave him a flirty look. "The great Danny Tremaine? Hunk of all hunks. Lover extraordinaire. With no holding power?"

Groaning, he left his shirt buttoned, tie only half undone and unzipped his fly as she lifted her skirt, stepped out of her panties and pushed him down into the chair behind him.

He grabbed her waist with both hands, lifted her on top of him as she spread her legs to bring them together. There was no finesse. No foreplay.

And no time.

Within seconds she was exploding around him, which set him off, coming inside her.

Collapsing against his chest, she started to giggle. His chuckle was weak but gained strength as each convulsion had them moving together down below.

"We're a pair, Doc. You ready for the ride?"

"God, yes."

"What do you say we get a flight to Vegas tonight? It's three hours earlier there, not that it matters, since it's the city that never sleeps. Marriage chapels are open all night."

"Vegas?"

"I want to marry you now. Tonight. If we don't get there by midnight to get the license, we can have the ceremony and tie up legalities in the morning."

Her heart jumped with excitement. And she was…her…with her mind spinning off toward consequences, ramifications, arrangements and…landing on… "But…"

"You want a wedding where both sets of our parents, and for you, stepparents, are all there for us to deal with at once?"

"I've got more junk here than you do. You make the reservations while I pack," she said, still seated on top of him, still holding him.

She felt him move. His arm. But it wasn't touching her. Curious, looking up, she saw his phone in his hand, while he scrolled, doing as she'd bid. Making reservations.

She kissed him. Knowingly. Wantingly. Full out with her whole heart.

And then she slid off him to go do her part.

She had to pack.

She'd never forget Milwaukee. Had conceived her first child there. Learned a lot. Grown up.

But life awaited, and she wasn't going to miss a second of it.

* * * * *

#2959 FORTUNE'S DREAM HOUSE

The Fortunes of Texas: Hitting the Jackpot • by Nina Crespo

For Max Fortune Maloney to get his ranch bid accepted, he has to convince his agent, Eliza Henry, to pretend they're heading for the altar. Eliza needs the deal to advance her career, but she fears jeopardizing her reputation almost as much as she does falling for the sweet-talking cowboy.

#2960 SELLING SANDCASTLE

The McFaddens of Tinsley Cove • by Nancy Robards Thompson

Moving to North Carolina to be a part of a reality real estate show was never in newly divorced Cassie Houston's plans but she needs a fresh start. That fresh start was not going to include romance—still, the sparks flying between her and fellow costar Logan McFadden are impossible to deny. But they both have difficult pasts and sparks might not be enough.

#2961 THE COWBOY'S MISTAKEN IDENTITY

Dawson Family Ranch • by Melissa Senate

While looking for his father, rancher Chase Dawson finds an irate woman. *How could he abandon her and their son?* The problem is, Chase doesn't have a baby. But he does have a twin. Chase vows to right his brother's wrongs and be the man Hannah Calhoun and his nephew need. Can his love break through Hannah's guarded heart?

#2962 THE VALENTINE'S DO-OVER

by Michelle Lindo-Rice

When radio personalities Selena Cartwright and Trent Moon share why they've sworn off love and hate Valentine's Day, the gala celebrating singlehood is born! Planning the event has Trent and Selena seeing, and wanting, each other more than just professionally. As the gala approaches, can they overcome past heartache and possibly discover that Trent + Selena = True Love 4-Ever?

#2963 VALENTINES FOR THE RANCHER

Aspen Creek Bachelors • by Kathy Douglass

Jillian Adams expected Miles Montgomery to propose—she got a breakup speech instead! Now Jillian is back, and their ski resort hometown is heating up! Their kids become inseparable, making it impossible to avoid each other. So when the rancher asks Jillian for forgiveness and a Valentine's Day dance, can she trust him, and her heart, this time?

#2964 WHAT HAPPENS IN THE AIR

Love in the Valley • by Michele Dunaway

After Luke Thornton shattered her heart, Shelby Bien fled town to become a jet-setting photographer. Shelby's shocked to find that single dad Luke's back in New Charles. When they join forces to fly their families' hot-air balloon, it's Shelby's chance at a cover story. And, just maybe, a second chance for the former sweethearts' own story!

HARLEQUIN PLUS

Try the best multimedia subscription service for romance readers like you!

Read, Watch and Play.

Experience the easiest way to get the romance content you crave.

Start your **FREE TRIAL** at
<u>www.harlequinplus.com/freetrial</u>.